The signs were indisputable— the boy was weakening

He'd been here four days ago, but Jarod wouldn't tell Laura. She was worried enough.

Jarod was worried himself. Tim Finlay'd had half a week to get into even worse trouble, and now a freeze was coming, a bad one.

He had to find Tim fast, and not just for the boy's sake. He had to do it for Gus. The sooner he got Laura back to Gus, the better.

She's his, Jarod's mind kept hissing at him. He had to remember that. He had no business thinking of her, watching her and liking what he saw. He steeled himself to ignore her.

Then he led her deeper into the wilderness.

Lisa Harris met her husband when he was hosting the local-television late show, "Fly By Night Movies." He was dressed as a giant housefly. Lisa was one of the show's writers and the props mistress. Her husband shed his fly suit to found his own film-and-video production company. Lisa now writes full-time and has published almost thirty novels—humor, romance and mystery. Despite her success, she still feels nostalgia for the days when "I had two hours to scrounge up a Mexican sombrero, a set of antique Colt revolvers and a horse that wouldn't spook when ridden by a giant fly!"

Watch for Lisa's Harlequin Temptation title in April. *Undercurrent* is part of the Passion's Quest promotion *and* it's the companion story to *I Will Find You!*

I WILL FIND YOU!
Lisa Harris

Harlequin Books

TORONTO • NEW YORK • LONDON
AMSTERDAM • PARIS • SYDNEY • HAMBURG
STOCKHOLM • ATHENS • TOKYO • MILAN
MADRID • WARSAW • BUDAPEST • AUCKLAND

To my wonderful Toronto Romance editors,
Debbie, Karin, Pat, Dianne, Paula and Laura

ISBN 0-373-03304-4

I WILL FIND YOU!

Copyright © 1994 by Lisa Harris.

CHAPTER ONE

LAURA FINLAY STOOD in the living room of the house that her great-grandfather had built more than a century ago. It was a quaint little house, and she'd often been told he'd purposely built it with such whimsy for one reason—so that it would always keep unhappiness away.

How ironic, Laura thought miserably. Unhappiness seemed to have settled in every corner. She pressed her forehead against the cold window and shut her eyes. She could not bear to look outside at the wintry rain-swept mountains.

Her own rash words kept haunting her. She flinched at the memory.

You, always you, she had flung at her younger brother. *Everything has to center on you. Don't you ever think I'd like a life of my own?*

It had been a stupid, terrible thing to say. Now Tim had run away, and the fault was hers.

Laura pushed her hand restlessly through her tumbled bangs. She was a small, pretty woman of twenty-seven. Usually her face was cheerfully pert and her hazel eyes danced with liveliness, but today her expression was shadowed by trouble.

Her most striking feature was her flame-red hair, short, curly and tousled. "A redhead through and through," her father used to say, for her feelings were easily touched and quickly roused.

Emotions, she thought shamefully. She wished she had none. If it hadn't been for her uncontrollable emotions, this disaster wouldn't have happened.

"Laura, did you even hear me?" her sister asked. "I said a tracker's coming. He can help. Really."

Startled, Laura tried to withdraw from her guilty reverie. She turned to her sister. "What?" she asked, pretending interest.

Susannah spoke again. "A tracker's coming. Not an amateur—a professional."

But the words barely registered with Laura. She drifted to the bookshelves and stared at her father's collection of religious books. He had been a minister. He had liked to sit in this snug little room to write his sermons. The coffee table had always been littered with his books, and soft music had played in the background.

She felt a pang of loss, remembering him. What would he have said in a case like this? "Heaven will provide," she supposed. But would heaven provide? And how?

"A tracker. His name is Jarod," Susannah said.

Laura shook her head. They had already had trackers. All had failed. Why should this one be different? "Jarod who?" she asked without enthusiasm. "From where?"

"Just Jarod," Susannah said impatiently. "He goes by one name, that's all."

Laura gave a shrug of indifference. "I don't trust people who only use one name." It was an irrelevant thing to say, but she was so depressed nothing made sense.

Susannah's voice hardened. "Laura, *listen* to me. Who cares about his name—if he can find Tim?"

Mention of Tim went through Laura as sharply as a spear. Abashed, she turned from the books, unable to meet her sister's eyes.

Tim, she thought in despair, *where are you? How are you? You've been gone for three days!*

She forced herself to look out the window. The February sky was pitilessly gray, and the cold rain steady. The Arkansas mountains stretched to the horizon, thick with dark pines and winter-bare trees.

The Spellbound Wilderness Area—once Laura had found the name comforting. Nature could flourish there, preserved from the rape of civilization.

Now the name sounded sinister, full of threat and untamed secrets. A man could die in the wilderness. Tim, vulnerable and alone, was out there somewhere, lost.

No, she amended, turning from the window: Tim was out there *hiding.* And maybe half-starved or hurt or unconscious or— She couldn't stand to think of the possibilities. They were too frightening.

She thought, instead, of the man called only Jarod. She looked at her sister unhappily. "All right. His name doesn't matter. He's really a professional. From around here?"

"No, but he's good," Susannah said earnestly. "One of the best."

Laura touched the rainbow-hued afghan on the couch. Once Tim had liked to curl up there, wrapped in this afghan, reading or writing. That was before everything had gone so completely wrong. "Where's he from? If not here?"

Susannah paused a moment. "Maine."

Laura eyed her sister in surprise. Maine? Maine was half a continent away from Arkansas. It had a different sort of country and climate altogether. Men who knew these mountains well had looked for Tim and failed. How could a stranger from faraway Maine do better?

Local searchers had found so little trace that one man swore Tim wasn't in the area at all.

The kid had probably hitchhiked to Hot Springs, the man said, and was safe in some hotel, while they were thanklessly freezing their butts off. After all, the man complained, who knew what a crazy kid like Tim might pull?

Laura had wanted to shake him. Tim *wasn't* crazy. And she knew, with an instinct deeper than reason, that he was somewhere in the wilderness. But even the search dogs hadn't been able to track him. Too much rain, their trainer said hopelessly.

Now it was down to this, Laura thought with fatalism. They would pin their hopes on a stranger who went, like a rock star, by one name. Maybe he could help. She hoped and prayed so, but she couldn't quite believe it.

Susannah went to the window and stared out. Reluctantly Laura's gaze followed her sister's. The wintry mountains seemed like enemies, holding them at bay. Laura had always loved this house and the beauty of its view. Until now, she had never known how ominous that same beauty could seem.

Laura moved to Susannah's side and put a hand on her shoulder. At first glance the two did not look like sisters. Susannah, twenty-five, was far taller and more reserved. She was slender, almost wandlike, with long auburn hair neatly swept back into a twist.

Her oversize horn-rimmed glasses made her look severe, although she was not. Susannah was the calm one, rational and steady with a quirky sense of humor. Laura was smaller and more femininely curved; she was usually the optimistic, outgoing one.

Their green-brown eyes, however, marked them as sisters. They had their late mother's eyes, large and longlashed. Their brother Tim, twenty-one, had them, too, and they helped make him a strikingly handsome young man. Like Laura, he was short but trim, with the body of a born athlete. His hair was curly like hers, but dark auburn like Susannah's.

Of the family's three children, Tim was the most gifted. Fate seemed to have given him everything—good looks, strength, intelligence, wit, warmth and charm.

In high school, Tim had shone as an honor student, a star athlete, an Eagle Scout. In college, he was the starting quarterback, vice president of his class and the youngest editor of the newspaper in the school's history. He had a double major, biology and journalism. He'd planned on being a scientist and nature writer.

Golden Boy, Susannah and Laura had used to tease him, laughing. And *Nature Boy.* From childhood he'd roamed the Spellbound area like a pilgrim exploring a sacred land. His sisters loved him without stint. How could one not love someone like Tim?

Laura bowed her head in frustration and rubbed her eyes. Tim had once had everything. Then, in one tragic moment, all changed.

It had happened almost a year and a half ago: a foggy autumn night on a twisting mountain road. Their father and Tim had been driving home from a fishing trip. The car blew a tire on a turn, crashed through a guardrail and plunged down the mountainside.

The crash had killed their father instantly, but Tim had been thrown free. Susannah and Laura had been grateful he was alive. He had a head injury, but they hadn't known then how complex, how exasperating, how soul-wrenching such an injury could be. There was not even time to come to terms with the loss of their father. Tim needed all their attention and energy if he was to recover.

Doctors said he might be almost as good as new—eventually. *Eventually* became the cruelest word Laura knew.

Tim's life had turned nightmarish. He quickly overcame most of his outward physical injuries. It was his inward invisible wounds that deviled him.

Tim was no longer himself, he was no longer *Tim*. An uncooperative stranger had seized control of his mind and body, and he hated it. He wanted his real self and his old life back.

Patience, everyone told him. But his temper had grown short-fused and fierce; patience was foreign to him.

He who had once written so beautifully could barely string two sentences together. His concentration was so erratic he could not read the poems and essays he once had written. The books he had loved had turned into puzzles whose secrets he could not penetrate.

College, for the time, was an impossibility. Football was forever out of the question. Tim, whose wit had been so quick, now had trouble finding his words. Friends who had come to see him were bewildered to find this angry, inarticulate, unpredictable stranger in his place. Their visits stopped.

It takes time, doctors told Tim repeatedly. All things come to those who wait. Rome wasn't built in a day.

Last Sunday night, Laura and Tim had been home alone together. Tim had been particularly contrary. He'd kept nagging Laura to drive him to Hot Springs, fifty miles away, to his favorite Mexican restaurant—because he was hungry for enchiladas.

There was plenty of food in the house, and Laura had been exhausted. She was a nurse at the hospital in the neighboring town of Corinth. She worked the night shift so she could spend days with Tim, and Sunday was her only night off. She adored Tim, but that night he had exasperated her.

She'd said no, she wasn't driving a round trip of a hundred miles because he had a silly whim for enchiladas. Tim had sworn at her—violently. Swearing was something he'd taken to lately because he sensed how much it grated on her nerves.

He'd pushed Laura past the edge, and her long pent-up frustration had exploded. "You—always you. Everything has to center on you! Don't you think I'd like a life of my own?"

She'd regretted her outburst immediately. The look on Tim's face had been one of naked pain.

He'd stalked to his room, slamming the door so hard the walls shook. Laura knew better than to try to apologize just then. She would wait until morning.

But when morning came, cold and misty, Tim was gone and so were his sleeping bag and his backpack. Laura and Susannah had searched the house frantically, then the two acres of wooded yard.

He was nowhere to be found. Laura and Susannah had looked first at each other, then out at the mountains stretching to the horizon, and they *knew:* he had run away.

Rain had begun to fall even as they stood there, looking at the fog-cloaked mountains. Laura had broken down and cried, sinking to her knees on the wet brown grass. Susannah drew her up, hugged her and walked her back to the house.

They'd called the sheriff's department. For three days parties had searched for Tim. The temperature was reassuringly mild during daylight, but hovered near freezing at night. And the rain kept falling.

Laura went out with the search party; of the two sisters, she was far more at home in the outdoors. She wanted to be on hand because doctors worried that Tim might panic if found by strangers. He might flee or resist them. Susannah stayed by the phone in case there was news.

But there was no news. Laura feared he was determined not to be found, and now, one by one, the volunteers who'd been searching were dropping out. Soon even the sheriff's department would give up; it could not spare its officers forever.

Laura's hand tightened on her sister's shoulder. For the thousandth time she wondered if Tim was hurt and helpless out in the wilderness.

Susannah turned and tried to give her an encouraging smile. She put her hand over Laura's. "This Jarod person will find him, Laura. I feel it."

"I hope so," Laura said. She gave Susannah's shoulder another squeeze, then moved toward the kitchen. She would make fresh coffee. How many cups had she drunk since Tim had left? A hundred? She was so full of caffeine her nerves jangled with it.

Susannah followed her. She took off her glasses and rubbed her eyes. Laura rinsed out the coffeepot and refilled it with fresh water.

"This tracker," Laura said, musing on the man again, "how'd you find him?"

Susannah seemed to falter. "Actually," she murmured, "he was...recommended. We're lucky he was free to come. And the good news is he'll be here soon."

Laura measured out the coffee. "How soon?"

"He's flying in tonight."

Laura looked at her in surprise. "Tonight? I'm sorry— I still can't believe it. It seems too much to hope for. But he's good? Really good?"

Susannah nodded. "Last year, in Minnesota, he found an autistic child who'd wandered into the woods. Everybody else had given up. She'd been gone six days when he started.

He found her in twenty hours. I'm told he's the best. He has excellent credentials.''

Laura fought down a growing sense of doubt. She'd been out in the mountains all afternoon, searching for Tim until rain had forced the party back. How, in that time, had Susannah discovered this mysterious miracle worker *and* convinced him to come to Arkansas? Could he really do any good? Hope warred with resignation in Laura's breast.

"It just doesn't seem possible," she said, still dubious. "Is he expensive? I mean, no price is too high, of course—"

"He won't charge anything."

Laura stared skeptically at her sister. "Nothing? But he's flying clear from Maine. Surely his airfare—"

"No," Susannah interrupted, turning away from Laura's scrutiny. "Nothing. He's charging nothing."

Laura put her hand on her hip. Susannah suddenly looked guilty. "You're saying he's a good Samaritan?" Laura persisted. "He's flying two thousand miles—out of the goodness of his heart?"

Susannah kept her back to her sister. She shrugged. "I was told . . . not to worry about money."

Laura's nerve ends prickled, sensing trouble. "Susannah, what's going on? He's getting here awfully fast. At no charge? Something's not right. You're holding out on me. How'd you find him?"

"I didn't exactly find him—myself, that is." She took off her big glasses and toyed with them. It was a habit she had when nervous. It was, Laura knew, nearly always a bad sign.

"Susannah," Laura demanded, "what do you mean?"

"I . . . I called Gus Raphael," Susannah said in a barely audible voice. She kept folding and unfolding the stems of her glasses.

Laura felt as if she'd been struck. "You *what?*" She took her sister by the elbow and wheeled her around to face her.

Susannah stared at the floor. "I called Gus Raphael," she repeated, but this time there was an edge of defiance in her tone. Her eyes met Laura's. "He knows about things like this—about missing people. He's got connections. He's worked with trackers before."

Laura's fatigue disappeared. Even her guilt and remorse vanished momentarily, replaced by a new dismay. "Gus is coming here, isn't he? You told him he could."

"Well..." Susannah started to say, then lifted one shoulder.

"Isn't he?"

"Yes," Susannah admitted, looking guiltier than ever.

Laura threw up her hands in a gesture of helpless exasperation. Lashing out at Tim had been the worst, the most shameful mistake of her life. But having been involved with Gus was the second worst, and the memory, she feared, would sting forever.

"How could you do this?" she pleaded. "How? Heaven knows everything's terrible enough—and now you're dragging Gus Raphael into it?"

Susannah jammed her glasses back on. She tossed her head rebelliously, and her eyes flashed. "Laura, he's bringing Jarod. It's for Tim's sake. You've got to understand that. We've got to put aside personal prejudice—"

"I hate that man," Laura said passionately. "I despise him. I never want to see him again."

"Well," Susannah challenged with equal passion, "do you want to argue about Gus? Or do you want to see Tim again?"

Laura drew her breath sharply. In exasperation she ran both hands through her hair. She had the panicky certainty that she was cornered.

"Susannah, you *know* what Gus did to me. He lied to me, misled me. He ruined my best friend's life. He ruined her family's life—"

Susannah's expression was adamant. "Tim, Laura. We're talking about Tim, not you."

"I'd do anything for Tim. But Gus? Why on earth did you call *him?*"

"I told you. He's with the FBI. He knows about these things—missing persons and such."

"He knows about missing *criminals*. He's from New York—he never even saw woods before he was twenty-two."

"He's resourceful," said Susannah.

"He's deceptive."

"He's a lawman, a . . . a specialist."

"He specializes in dirty tricks."

"Laura, it's his job. He couldn't help lying to you. He was on assignment. He was undercover."

Laura refused to be pacified. "He ruined *lives*. The lives of people I loved."

Susannah raised her chin and looked almost righteous. "Maybe he did and maybe he didn't. It's beside the point. Right now there's a life to save— Tim's."

Laura, half-sickened, shook her head. "Gus would exploit any situation, including this."

"He's doing this because he cares for you. He wants to make up for what happened. And he *is* bringing Jarod. That's what's important here—the tracker. If the tracker can find Tim, I don't care who brings him—even the devil himself," she said and then left the room.

It is the devil himself, Laura thought darkly. *He's coming back to play games again. And this time what's at stake is my brother's life.*

She turned from the coffeemaker, forgetting to switch it on. She found herself staring out the kitchen window. Night was falling fast. The rain poured, steady and sinister.

She closed her eyes and sent a prayer to Tim. She hoped he was safe and warm and fed. But she feared for him with all her heart.

Then she thought of Gus Raphael. She remembered the whole business in Hot Springs; how blithely Gus had lied and how many lives he had wrecked. He'd defended himself, saying it was for the sake of justice. She'd been appalled. She'd said there was no excuse for such deceit; the end could not possibly justify the means.

For Tim's sake alone would she agree to see Gus. She was about to let the devil walk through her door again only because he'd promised to bring a delivering angel with him.

Jarod, she thought with foreboding, *you'd better be worth this.*

JAROD COULD TELL Gus was restless. But then, Gus had been born restless. Jarod pitied him. He pitied any man who thought himself in love.

Jarod had small faith in women or in humanity as a whole. He was a private man, a bit shy, who felt most comfortable staying aloof and relying only on himself. He allowed few people into his circle of friendship. Gus was one.

Jarod folded his arms and stared out the window of the rented sedan. Its headlights sliced through the night, illuminating the wet twists of the road.

He sat slouched in the passenger seat, looking as relaxed as a lounging cat. He was just under six feet tall, and he had a runner's spare body, hard with lean muscle.

He had high cheekbones, an elegantly hawklike nose, a disciplined mouth and a lean jaw. His eyes, under dark brows, were the mysterious gray of smoked crystal. The eyes alone kept his face from being severe. They were beautiful, but they gave him the unsettling air of a man who saw things invisible to others.

His hair was dark, slightly wavy and shoulder-length. He kept it tied back with a strip of rawhide. Around his wrist was a beaded bracelet.

He wore faded jeans and a pair of fringed brown leather boots that came halfway to his knees. Around his throat was a necklace of beads and small shells. It had been given to him by his part-Indian friend and teacher, old Raymond Hare.

Jarod's dark green flannel shirt was well-worn. A long mottled feather hung from a beaded thong tied to one button. His only concession to fashion was a relatively new down-filled vest of navy blue. It wasn't, apparently, concession enough for Gus, who was something of a dandy.

Gus cast him a critical glance. "Don't you own any street clothes?" he grumbled. "And I wish you'd get your hair cut. Frankly, you don't make a good impression."

Jarod's only reply was a yawn. He knew it would annoy Gus, and Gus, annoyed, was entertaining.

"The haircut," continued Gus. "The haircut is definitely retro. That is not a haircut designed to inspire confidence. There's a woman involved in this who I want to impress."

Jarod gazed up at the dark sky, trying to guess the time without seeing the stars. He figured it was 8:03 in the evening. He glanced at the dashboard clock: 8:04.

"If you want to impress her, impress her," he said in a lazy voice. "She's got nothing to do with me."

"Wrong," Gus said emphatically. "We had—" he made a deprecatory gesture "—a tiff. You're my peace offering. A gift so to speak. You should be wrapped better."

Gus was a dark intense man, taller and even leaner than Jarod. His looks were Hispanic, as was his slight accent, and there was usually a mocking twist to both his mouth and the words that came out of it.

Jarod didn't smile often, but Gus's sardonic manner usually amused him. The corner of his mouth turned up slightly. "I can't believe it. The same woman you were trying to get back two years ago? She's still mad? That you lied—in the line of duty?"

"Yes," Gus admitted irritably. He gave Jarod a suspicious sidelong glance. "When did I tell you about the...lies? I don't remember telling you that part."

Jarod yawned again. "In the swamp. Where else?"

"Oh, my God, the swamp," Gus said in disgust. "In the swamp I could have babbled out my whole life story."

"You did. But so what? We got your man."

Two years ago, the bureau had called in Jarod on one of Gus's cases. Gus's suspect, Etienne Tussard, a smuggler with a Cajun background, had fled into the Florida Everglades.

Jarod, Gus, two other federal agents and two Florida state policemen set out after him. The other federal men couldn't keep the pace Jarod had set. Then one of the police officers got sick and dropped out. Finally the second quit from sheer exhaustion. Jarod and Gus alone tracked Tussard for more than a hundred tortuous miles.

Jarod fought back a grin, remembering some of the more absurd episodes of that grueling journey. At the outset, Gus had seemed the least likely man to make it through the Everglades. Jarod had taken one look at his cuff links and silk tie and figured he'd be the first one to drop out. He'd figured wrong.

No matter how harsh the conditions, Gus didn't quit. He was the most dauntless SOB Jarod had ever encountered, and Jarod respected him for it.

"But this time you've got to sit out," Jarod said, shaking his head at the recollections. "You don't have to go."

"I want to. I *can't.*" Gus pointed at his own left foot. "I was shot, remember? I'm supposed to stay off this foot. You go into the mountains, get the kid. I'll stay behind. And comfort the women."

"You'd better not tell them how you got shot."

"Why?" Gus demanded. "I got shot in the line of duty is how I got shot."

"With your own gun," Jarod taunted lackadaisically. "You shot yourself in the foot with your own gun."

"I did not. I was in a struggle—did I say a life-and-death struggle? It was. The gun went off. I did *not* shoot myself."

Jarod knew, but only smiled.

"Besides," Gus said, "she's really crazy for me. Deep down, she wants me back. She's a very idealistic woman. I offended her principles and hurt her pride. But she wants me to come after her."

"That's why she hasn't spoken to you for two years."

Gus made a dismissive gesture. "Look, the rest of her family forgave me. Her sister always talks to me when I phone. Her sister *likes* me, she's pulling for me. Even her brother said he saw my side. Hey, when we get there, take her aside. Tell her how wonderful I am."

"That should take all of two seconds."

"I'm serious. And I'm counting on you to deliver for me. She loves this brother. He's the apple of her eye. I don't blame her. She took me home a couple of times—before our little, uh, misunderstanding. He's a good kid, a great kid. But then he had this accident. You gotta bring him back in one piece."

Jarod's smile faded. "I can't make promises. You know that." In the darkness he could barely make out the low mountains, but he could tell they were different from the ones in the East.

He could sense that difference sharply. Feel that ancient secrets slept in these hills, and subtle dangers dwelt among them.

"This place can pull tricks," he said, half to himself.

"Don't let it pull tricks on you, that's all," Gus said. "Look, you get feelings, right? What do you feel about her brother? Is he okay? In trouble? What?"

Gus didn't say the word that haunted Jarod: *dead*. Maybe the kid had gone into the woods in order to die. Jarod shrugged, troubled. "I've got no feelings, one way or another. Except this . . . uneasiness."

"Uneasiness?" Gus said, a frown line appearing between his eyes. "I don't like that. The woman I'm talking about—her sun rises and sets on that kid. She *loves* him."

Jarod stared at the windshield wipers moving hypnotically back and forth. Always, before he began a search, a sort of picture came into his mind, unbidden. He disliked calling it a vision, but knew of no other name for it.

The vision was of the person he sought, of what condition that person would be in when found. Sometimes the image was clear, sometimes dim, but it was never wrong.

When he'd gone after the autistic child, he'd known she'd be weak, but alive. When he and Gus had gone after Tussard in the Everglades, he knew they would find him full of fight. And when he'd set out last summer after the elderly man in the White Mountains of New Hampshire, he'd been certain from the start, and rightly so, that the old man was already dead.

But when he thought of searching for Tim Finlay, no vision came. None. Jarod didn't know what it meant.

He fingered a small deerskin bag on the end of his necklace. It contained a few simple objects that had meaning only to him. "Mojo power," Gus had gibed during their long slog through the swamp.

Jarod didn't know what to call the force that guided him, but he didn't joke about it, and he didn't doubt it. Something was telling him that the Finlay search would be different. But how? And why?

He could have sworn, for an instant, that the mountains around him were whispering secrets.

"You really love this woman—after all this time?" he asked suddenly, surprised by his own words. He and Gus seldom talked of emotions, and then only with an edge of humor. And he himself avoided speaking of love. He distrusted the word.

"What?" Gus said. "What is this? A quiz? A test?" But then he was silent a moment, staring into the darkness. "Yeah," he said. "Yeah. I love her. Why do you think I'm dragging you down here, you idiot? Because I'm indifferent to her?"

Jarod lifted one brow in disinterest. "Forget it. I don't know why I asked. She sounds hard-hearted, that's all."

"You don't know her. She's anything but hard-hearted. And I'm not ashamed—I can't get her out of my system. I'm sorry her brother's in trouble, and I'm sorry the only way I can get to see her is by hauling you along with me. But if that's what it takes..." He shrugged unhappily.

When Gus spoke again, his tone was full of bitterness and regret. "I hate it. I hate capitalizing on her trouble. I hate having to trust this to you. I wish I could do it myself. I'd do anything for her. But I can't. I've got to trust you."

Jarod fingered the deerskin bag again. *Trust*. In the Everglades, Gus had trusted him with his very life.

Once they closed in on Tussard, Jarod had relied on Gus in return. Tussard was desperate. Jarod never used a gun, so when the smuggler opened fire, it was up to Gus to stop him. Then together they'd lugged the wounded man back toward civilization, fighting to keep him alive. And they'd done it.

The bond between Gus and Jarod was deep, if unspoken. It was the bond of men who have depended on each other, who have faced death together.

"There's no buddy like your foxhole buddy," old Raymond Hare, a veteran of Korea, had once told Jarod. Jarod had never been to war, but after the Everglades, he understood.

Jarod was a loner, but he had his loyalties, and they were strong. Now that old Raymond was gone, Jarod supposed Gus was the man he liked and respected most. This was only the third time they'd seen each other since their odyssey through the swamp, but that didn't matter. What mattered was Jarod liked Gus and trusted him implicitly.

Hell, if Gus thought getting this woman would make him happy, Jarod would do what he could. One way or the other, he'd find the kid. He just hoped he'd find him alive.

As for the woman—the little fool—maybe she'd wise up and appreciate Gus for what he was. Then Gus could marry her and, poor chump, discover to his dismay that she was just an ordinary mortal like anybody else.

Maybe he'd even manage to be tolerably happy with her. If not, if it didn't work, at least he'd have her out of his system.

Once again Jarod felt grudging pity for his friend. Experience had taught him that love was a madness, a means of turning an otherwise sane man into a fool. He thanked God that he had become immune. But he also envied Gus—just a little.

It must be nice to want something that much, Jarod thought idly. It might be almost...interesting to feel that deeply once again.

No, he told himself with conviction. He had sworn off such false and foolish pleasures. He was detached from the mainstream of human life and determined to remain so. He could not even imagine the woman who could make him feel otherwise.

CHAPTER TWO

LAURA'S HEART LURCHED when the knock rattled the door. She knew it was Gus Raphael. And the man called Jarod, of course. She wouldn't allow Gus in the house at all if it weren't for the tracker.

Susannah answered the door because Laura could not bring herself to do it. She stood behind her father's armchair nervously clutching its back as if for protection.

Her spine stiffened as soon as she saw Gus. He hadn't changed. He was as dapper as ever, as tall, as slim. His face had the same combination of asceticism and sensuality, the hollow cheeks, the full lips and hooded eyes.

"Susannah," he said to her sister, his voice full of compassion. "I'm so sorry about this...about your trouble." He put an arm around Susannah and gave her a brotherly peck on the cheek.

And Susannah *let* him. Laura, resentful, clenched the chair's back more tightly.

"And Laura," Gus said, moving toward her, his arms out. He limped slightly and had a cast on his left foot. "As soon as I heard I had to come."

She disliked his glib words, his elegant clothes. And how arrogant he was! Did he imagine she'd greet him with open arms?

"Don't touch me," she said, and meant it with all her heart.

Gus stopped. He made an accommodating gesture, then let his arms drop to his sides. He didn't have the decency to look abashed. His expression was annoyingly sympathetic.

"Laura," he said again. "Are you all right? My heart's been with you."

She didn't reply. She held his gaze, her heart pounding with animosity.

"It's all right," he said gently, "I've brought someone to help— Jarod." He nodded back toward the doorway.

For the first time, Laura noticed the other man, who had entered behind Gus. A pair of startlingly clear gray eyes met hers. Her heart lurched again.

She hadn't known what to expect of the tracker. Mentally she'd conjured up a burly Maine lumberjack with a black beard, plaid shirt and knit watchcap. This man was lean and clean-shaven, with nothing of the lumberjack about him. He looked like a cross between an angel and a savage. There was something otherworldly in those beautiful eyes, but at the same time their expression seemed implacable, relentless.

He had an aquiline nose, high cheekbones, an angular jaw and stubborn chin. The line of his mouth was disciplined, almost forbidding. His brows were darker than his hair, which was brown streaked with gold. It was longer than Laura's own and drawn back severely.

His flannel shirt and faded jeans seemed ordinary enough, but his fringed boots came halfway to his knees and were crisscrossed with leather ties. A strange necklace of beads and shells hung around his throat and disappeared inside his forest-green shirt.

From one shirt button hung a single feather fastened by a beaded strip of leather. He carried a bedroll over one shoulder and a well-worn backpack in his other hand.

Susannah stood staring at him, her eyes wide behind her glasses.

"Hello," said Jarod. He had a deep voice, and it sent odd sensations scampering up Laura's back. Her mouth was suddenly dry.

"Hello," she said with forced civility. "I'm Laura Finlay, and this is my sister, Susannah."

Jarod glanced at Susannah, then turned his startling eyes back to Laura. "I've come to find your brother. I'd start tonight if I knew the country better. As soon as the sun's up, I'll go."

Laura felt as if a giant fist had squeezed all air from her lungs. "We're . . . very grateful. Of course I'll be going with you."

"No!" Gus objected. He looked first at Laura, then at Jarod, then back at Laura. "That's out of the question."

Amazingly Laura had temporarily forgotten Gus was there. She gazed at him with surprise, then resentment. "One of us needs to go," she told him impatiently. "The doctors said Tim might not let a stranger near him. The sheriff said the same thing. Tim's no longer . . . logical. He may think that we're searching for him to punish him."

For a moment the other three stared at Laura in silence. "I go alone," Jarod said at last, the set of his mouth more obdurate than before. "You'd slow me down. Time's important. A cold spell's coming."

He sounded so sure of himself that the back of Laura's neck prickled. "That's not the forecast. The temperature's supposed to stay above freezing."

"The forecast is wrong," Jarod said.

Oh, good heaven, he's as arrogant as Gus, Laura thought in despair. With his feathers and beads, he looked as if he'd stepped out of an earlier century—and he had the outmoded male chauvinism to match.

"Right or wrong, I'm going." She folded her arms to show him she meant business.

"Laura, you can't—" Gus insisted. "I forbid it. You don't even know this man."

Laura shot him a fiery look that told him he had no right to forbid her anything. "I'm certainly not staying here with *you.*"

"Miss Finlay," Jarod said in his low voice, "you don't understand. When I go into those mountains, I won't come out until I've found your brother. I travel fast, I travel hard. This is no Girl Scout camping trip."

"He's right," Gus said emphatically. "He goes at a killer pace. *I* could hardly keep up with him."

"I can keep up with Tim," Laura said with a toss of her head. She gave Jarod a defiant glance. "And I can keep up with you."

"I go alone," Jarod said. The expression was cold, almost hostile.

Susannah stepped forward, adjusting her glasses with a scholarly air. "The psychiatrist said one of us should be available—immediately—if needed. So did Dr. Thatcher. So did the sheriff."

She held her head higher. "If you're an expert, you know they're right. Tim isn't lost. He's hiding. And his thinking, unfortunately, isn't straight. He's probably suffering from fatigue and exposure, which'll make it worse."

She looked Jarod up and down. "In addition, your appearance is a bit off-putting. It's not likely Tim will show himself to some stranger dripping with beads and elk teeth or whatever."

Laura took a deep breath, then held it. Susannah had sounded as assured as a professor. Laura could see the displeased conflict etched on Jarod's lean countenance. He gave Susannah a long measuring look.

"All right," he said at last, nodding at Susannah. "If I have to take somebody, I'll take you."

"Fine," Gus said, holding up his hands as if everything was settled. "You make sense, Susannah. You've always been a very reasonable woman. You go with Jarod. I'll stay here and care for Laura."

Susannah stepped backward, shaking her head. "No. We settled this before you came. We agreed. Laura goes."

"Ahh," Gus said sagely, "but you're the calm, rational, prudent one, Susannah. Always sure to keep a cool head in a crisis. Who's better suited than you to—"

"Gus, please!" Laura said in exasperation. "It's decided. I'm better in the woods than Susannah. I always have been."

"It's true," Susannah agreed. "I'm the bookworm, not the athlete."

"I'd rather have you," Jarod told her, his expression grim.

Susannah seemed alarmed by his intensity. She swallowed and shook her head. "Laura goes," she said.

"No," Gus said. "No, no, *no!*"

"Yes," Laura said, standing straighter. Jarod flashed her a daunting look, but she met his eyes and held them.

"You've got yourself a traveling companion, Mr. Jarod," she said crisply. "Whether you like it or not."

His crystal gray gaze seemed to pierce her through, but she refused to flinch.

AT BEDTIME, Jarod asked to use Tim's room so he could understand him better.

Sitting at Tim's desk, he'd studied the maps of the wilderness area Laura had given him. They'd been made by the state university's geology department. They gave him a general picture, but not a detailed one.

He memorized the main features of the land. He imagined the paths, both logical and illogical, that Tim might take. What would the kid be most likely to do? Where would his emotions drive him—and why?

Jarod browsed through Tim's collection of woodlore references, the books the boy could no longer read, and thought he found a clue there, a good one.

At last he lay on Tim's bed, still fully clothed, his eyes closed. He focused his thoughts on Tim as intently as he could. His mind, like a phantom fox, ran first one imaginary path, then another. He tried to submerge his own identity within the boy's.

Then Gus burst in without knocking and broke his trance.

Jarod opened his eyes. The look on Gus's face was one of unspeakable frustration. He shut the door, then jerked out the chair from Tim's desk and sat, propping his bad foot on the bed.

"You're ruining my concentration," Jarod muttered.

"You're ruining my life," Gus retorted. "Sit up. Stop that voodoo."

Jarod gave a harsh sigh and straightened, leaning against the headboard. He folded his arms and gazed at Gus, his face impassive. "It's not voodoo. I'm not ruining your life. I did what I could do to keep her from going."

"Sneak off without her," Gus ordered. "Before the sun comes up."

Jarod threw him a sidelong glance, his mouth grim. "They're right. I know they're right. That kid with autism. I took her uncle with me. She didn't want to come with me. I scared her—she wanted to hide as soon as she saw me."

"So take an uncle this time."

Jarod lifted a critical eyebrow. "Is there an uncle?"

"No," Gus admitted.

"Then I take the woman. We've got no choice."

"You're out in the woods with my woman, and I sit here with Susannah. You know what Susannah's idea of a good time is? A bracing game of chess. Take her. Leave my woman with me, where she belongs."

Jarod put his hands behind his head again and stared at the ceiling. "Your woman is safe. I don't want her. One of them has to go, and the tall one won't. Besides, the little one's a nurse. You didn't tell me that. It might help. Anyway, I think the tall one's better-looking."

"Don't denigrate the woman I love."

"I'm not. We have different tastes, that's all."

Gus sighed, and Jarod kept staring at the ceiling. In truth he was troubled. He'd been honest; he thought Susannah was the prettier sister, even with her owllike glasses.

But Laura... At last he understood Gus Raphael's fascination. She was more curvaceous, more natural, certainly more vivacious than her sister.

She had extraordinary spirit; she practically radiated it. Although she was not a true beauty, her eyes had struck him—and held him. They flashed with such life that they transformed a pretty face into a mesmerizing one.

She seemed, unlike Jarod, so *connected* to her emotions. Even when she'd rebuked Gus, she did it with such wide-eyed, sincere energy it had an unexpected charm to it.

She lived in this elflike little house at the edge of the woods, and she seemed sort of enchanted herself—all fire and quicksilver and undiluted feeling.

Yes, he thought uneasily, he could see why she'd gotten to Gus, seen all too clearly.

"This girl," Gus said, "she's been like a...a sword through my heart for two years. I can't let her go with you alone. I'll go, too."

With a sound of exasperation, Jarod sat up straighter, swinging his legs over the edge of the bed. He leaned his elbows on his knees and stared pointedly at Gus's wounded foot. "You can't. I move fast. You hobble."

"I'll hobble fast."

"You're supposed to stay off that foot. We'll be going for miles. You want to gimp yourself up permanently?"

Gus made a slight grimace. He shook his head. "Look, what bothers me is this. You and I went after Tussard. It took us five days and four nights to catch up with him. I can't stand the idea of your spending nights with her. It's maddening is what it is."

"I said don't worry. She's all yours. She's safe with me. I give you my word."

"She's extremely attractive. Some people don't realize it at first. The first time I saw her I thought she was cute, but ordinary. But then she smiled, and I thought, *Estoy loco por ti. ¿Quieres venir, y veras mis tatuajes?*"

Jarod frowned. "You felt crazy for her? You wanted to show her your tattoos?"

"It was a polite way of saying I yearned to take off my clothes."

"Did it ever occur to you that maybe you're a little too...intense?"

"She *liked* my intensity. She told me so."

"So what changed?" Jarod asked sardonically.

"I told you. She found out I lied a little."

Jarod was dubious. "You never said exactly how much of what you told her was a lie. How much?"

"About—" Gus shrugged "—a hundred percent. But only facts. Never feelings. Tell her that. I never lied about feelings. Tell her that I'm a good guy, okay? Tell her I'm a prince of a fellow?"

Jarod looked at him, surprised at how pained Gus seemed. He had it bad, all right. Jarod knew that feeling; once, long ago, he'd had it himself. It was like dying without being able to fall down. *Oh, hell,* he wanted to say to Gus, *no woman's worth it. Not even this one.*

"I'll tell her you're a good guy," he said, instead. "I'll tell her you're a prince of a fellow."

Gus became somber again. "And you keep your hands off her, *comprende?*"

"*Comprende,*" Jarod agreed. "I won't touch her. I swear it."

"And you'll speak on my behalf?"

Jarod nodded. "I'll speak on your behalf. I'll figure out something good to say—somehow. Now get out. Let me think."

Gus stood. He gave Jarod a soft punch in the shoulder, a gesture of grudging affection. "You're all right," he said. "Good luck out there."

Jarod nodded but didn't look at the other man. He wasn't used to emotion from Gus. He wasn't used to it from anyone. It embarrassed him.

As soon as Gus was gone, Jarod stretched out on Tim's bed again, trying to concentrate. With his right hand he touched the medicine bag that hung from his necklace.

Where are you, kid? How are you? How will you be when I find you?

Nothing but featureless mist swarmed in his mental vision. He gritted his teeth, but the mist only grew thicker, darker.

Then for a moment, he glimpsed something clearly—a pair of beautiful green-brown eyes aswim with tears. His heart turned over. He recognized those eyes and knew they weren't the boy's. They were Laura Finlay's. What her tears might mean, he didn't know. But they gave him a hollow feeling in his chest and an unexpected tightening in his groin.

Don't think about her, he warned himself fiercely, appalled by his involuntary response.

He'd given Gus his word. He never broke his word or made a vow he didn't keep. His code was that simple—and that absolute.

Finding Laura attractive was a sort of unwilling treachery. He himself had been on the receiving end of the betrayal of love. The memory of it, even after all these years, filled him with bitterness and made a taste like wormwood lodge in his throat.

He would never betray a friend, especially for a woman. On such matters he was inflexible. He kept his life Spartan, his emotions in check, and he held his honor as dearly as he held his life.

ALL NIGHT LONG, Laura had nightmares. In her dreams she saw Tim in pain and danger. She awoke when the sky was still black and knew she would not fall back to sleep.

She rose, put on her robe and padded to the kitchen, glad for the silence of the sleeping house, grateful for the solitude it offered. She had to steel herself for the arduous task of keeping up with Jarod.

The small light over the stove was on. She and Susannah had kept it burning lately; one of them always seemed to be waking up in the middle of the night. It cast just enough light to see by.

She reached for the coffeemaker and found it already full of coffee, hot and fresh.

She wheeled, startled to see Jarod seated at the table in the semidarkness, holding a cup of coffee and staring at her. Even in the shadows, she could feel the force of his clear-eyed gaze.

"Oh!" she gasped. "What are you doing here?"

"Thinking." His gray eyes didn't waver, and the deepness of his voice sent a frisson rippling through her.

"Thinking?"

"About your brother."

"Oh." Laura looked away from him, self-conscious at being seen in her short pajamas and old blue robe. She pulled the robe tightly shut and tied the knot in its belt more firmly. She took a coffee mug out of the cupboard and filled it.

She didn't sit down across from Jarod. Instead, she leaned against the counter. Nervously, she sipped the coffee.

In the half-light, he looked even more hawklike than she'd remembered. He wore the same dark shirt, its sleeves rolled halfway up his forearms. He wore a bracelet of braided leather and beads around his left wrist.

"You'd better eat," he said without emotion. "It's your last chance at the comforts of civilization for a while."

For a while. The phrase had an ominous ring.

"How long will it take to find him?" Laura asked. "Do you have any idea?"

"No. You should eat. I mean it."

She shivered. The idea of food repelled her, but she supposed she should offer him something. The rain had stopped, but it would be cold in the mountains; they would burn a lot of energy.

"I'll fix you something," she said, opening the refrigerator. "Are eggs all right?"

"Don't bother. Please."

"It's no bother," she said, anxious to do something, do anything. She was too aware of this man, and it unsettled her.

"No. I don't eat beforehand."

She turned, giving him a look of wary curiosity. "You tell me to eat, but you won't?"

"No."

"You mean you fast? Is that some sort of...ceremony or something?"

"No. Just a habit."

"Oh." She closed the refrigerator door.

"But you should have something," he said.

"No. I don't want to eat, either. Every time I do, it sticks in my throat. I think of Tim. I wonder if he's hungry. If he's cold. If he's scared. In pain. In . . . trouble of some kind."

Jarod kept watching her with his same disconcerting steadiness. "Gus says the kid knows what he's doing in the woods."

Gus. Laura shuddered. He'd barely crossed her mind. She pushed away even the mere idea of him and thought of her brother, instead.

"Tim *used* to know what he was doing," she said unhappily. "He knew that stretch of forest better than anybody I ever saw. But now . . . Who can say? I don't know how well he can take care of himself. That's why I'm so worried."

"We're going to find him," Jarod said. He spoke flatly, without bravado, as if it was already an accomplished fact.

She looked at him dubiously. "You're very sure of yourself."

"Yes."

She lifted her chin. "But what shape do you suppose he'll be in? I keep imagining . . ." She didn't finish the sentence. No words came, and she was ashamed to realize tears had welled in her eyes, stinging. Angry at the sign of weakness, she wiped them away.

He set down his coffee mug. He rose from the table and came to her side. His dark brows were drawn together in a frown of perplexity. "We'll find him. That's all I can promise. Are you all right?"

"Of course I'm all right," she protested, but she knew she wasn't. She felt exhausted in both body and spirit by her fears for Tim, and she was running on sheer willpower. She braced herself, trying to draw on deeper reserves.

She wiped her hand across her eyes again, obliterating the last trace of her tears. "The sun'll be up in a few minutes. Are you ready to go?"

"Yes. And you?"

"I . . . I packed my gear as soon as I knew you were coming. All I have to do is change my clothes."

"Can you travel light?"

"Very."

He smiled sardonically. It was the first time she could recall seeing him smile. He had a deep dimple in his left cheek, which startled her because it was so unexpected.

"I mean it," she said, resenting what his smile implied. "I don't tromp off into the woods carrying a hair dryer and eighteen bottles of nail polish. I'm not carrying canned hams and jars of mayonnaise."

His smile faded. "Your brother. What did he take? Tell me again. Have you remembered anything else?"

She shrugged in frustration. They had been through this last night. "A change of clothes. His sleeping bag. An ax, knife, canteens—the usual gear. But no tent. And the jacket he took was light. Too light."

"Food?"

Laura shook her head. "Some dry soup. Tea bags. Granola bars. Not much, really. Not enough for all the time he's been gone."

"There's food out there for the taking," Jarod said. "Can he live off the land?"

She bit her lip. "He *could.* I don't think he ever actually *did* for more than a day a time. And since the accident, what he still knows and doesn't is all . . . mixed-up. I keep worrying. If he's hungry, if he's light-headed, he could get terribly confused. He could get hurt. He could . . ."

Once more she was unable to finish. "Oh, God," she said, and the words were a desperate prayer.

Jarod stood watching her. She struggled to keep her expression tightly controlled. He himself looked troubled, which did not help her confidence.

"Change your clothes," he said with surprising gentleness.

HE DIDN'T HAVE to wait long.

She reappeared in the kitchen promptly, shrugging her arms into the straps of her backpack. He was surprised at her quickness, her efficiency, and how she had wrestled down her emotions to achieve a hard-won composure.

She wore a dark blue parka, a blue knit cap and black leather gloves. Her hiking boots were good ones, well-worn. Her tumble of red curls peeked from beneath the cap, and the look in her beautiful green-brown eyes was of fierce determination.

"Let's go," she said, wriggling her shoulders to fit more snugly against the pack. She gave a little toss of her chin.

He stared down at her, an odd lump in his throat, and once again understood why Gus hadn't been able to get her out of his system. The longer he looked at her the prettier she seemed. Hadn't Gus said the same thing?

Guiltily he glanced away. "Don't you want to say goodbye to your sister?" he asked. "And Gus?"

"Gus," she said contemptuously. "I don't want to say hello or goodbye or anything else to him. As for Susannah, let her sleep. She needs it, poor thing."

He shifted the weight of his pack. He could survive quite well without it and move faster, but when he searched for someone, he had to be ready for whatever he found. Food, dry clothes, a first-aid kit—he had them all if the kid needed them.

"I've got the radio," Laura said. "My own food, everything."

He nodded. Last night she'd told him about the radio the sheriff's department had given her. The department could fly in a helicopter for Tim if needed. Normally no machinery was allowed in the wilderness area. The only exception was a medical emergency. Jarod hoped they wouldn't find one.

His own parka was stuffed into his backpack in case Tim needed it. Jarod was used to cold and could make do with the down vest. He also wore a broad-brimmed black hat pulled low over his eyes. A long knife with a beaded sheath hung from his belt and was strapped to his thigh. It was the only weapon he ever took with him.

"Do you have the maps?" Laura asked, worry haunting her eyes.

He shook his head. "We don't need them," he said. He tapped his temple. "They're here."

"But you've never actually *seen* any of this. Don't you think we should—"

"You've got to trust me."

"Trust you," she said, doubt in her voice.

"Yes."

She looked at him for a long taut moment.

He had a stab of awareness so sharp it momentarily cut off his breath. *My God,* he thought, *those eyes are beautiful.*

He had seldom been stared down, but he glanced away quickly, unhappy that he had looked at the woman Gus loved and felt an undeniable surge of desire.

"Trust you," she repeated, then breathed, "All right. I'll follow you as far as I have to go."

He said nothing. A muscle flicked in his cheek. He did not look at her again. His only answer was a brusque nod.

Together they set off from the house in the faint gray light of early dawn.

CHAPTER THREE

WHEN HE STARTED, he traveled so quickly that Laura had to struggle to match his pace. But she kept up with him, her mouth clamped tight.

Half a mile from the house, he headed south, plunging down the mountain and through a deep vine-choked gorge.

No path offered itself. The terrain humped and dipped beneath their feet, and underbrush blocked their way. The gorge was so unlikely a route to take that no one had ever bothered to investigate it.

The way was choked with obstacles. Nobody, the other searchers had reasoned, would fight his way down that steep-sided brambly ravine.

But Jarod seemed to find signs of the opposite, and his eyes gleamed with knowing satisfaction. His concentration was so complete that he fascinated her—and frightened her. He was, after all, seeing the unseeable. What had been invisible to others was clear to him.

She followed him without question. He picked his steps carefully and made no sound in the dense brush.

She tried to follow in his footsteps, but twigs cracked, vines clutched at her shins and caught her ankles. Once a bramble snagged her so hard that her jeans tore, and she knew she must be bleeding. She didn't stop to check.

She felt blundering and awkward compared to him, and she looked at him with growing respect. There was such rightness in his every move, which struck her as positively mysterious.

He took an odd dodging path that only he could see. Instead of cutting across the ravine to easier ground, he stayed in the narrow valley, following its tortuous meandering.

At last, he paused, then with no explanation changed course and began to climb the sheerest slope of the gorge. The ascent veered so steeply that often Laura had to drag herself up by grabbing at roots and branches.

Once she could find no handhold and nearly panicked. *I won't ask for help,* she thought. *If I ask for help, he'll think I'm slowing him down.*

Yet Jarod turned, just as if she had spoken to him. His eyes didn't meet hers, but he stretched his arm toward her, offering his hand.

Heated by walking, she had long ago stripped off her gloves and hat. Her bare hand locked with his. It was the first time they had touched, and an unwarranted shock of awareness shot through her body.

His grip was so certain that when he drew her up to the next handhold, she felt as if she'd been brought aloft by a supernatural force. Then his hand released hers. She felt earthbound again, an ordinary mortal.

He stopped two-thirds of the way up the face of the ravine when a ledge of limestone jutted above them. He raised himself to it, then crouched there as surely poised as a cat, studying the mottled gray rock.

Laura drew herself up beside him and sat, struggling not to pant. She glanced at her watch. They had been on the move for three and a half hours, and she was grateful to rest, even for a minute. She looked at Jarod in puzzlement, not knowing what he stared at so intently.

He rose. He gazed down at her and nodded to the south. Sighing, Laura started to get to her feet. But the pack was heavy, her legs rubbery, and she stumbled slightly. For a moment she feared she would fall, awkward and flailing, down the treacherous slope of the ravine.

Jarod's arm shot out and he caught her by the elbow. For a moment she hung, teetering helplessly, on the edge of the stone shelf. His other hand gripped her firmly by the strap of her pack and pulled her back to safety.

Fighting the weight of the pack, she could regain her balance only by leaning against him. Briefly her face touched the warm hardness of his shoulder. His chin grazed her hair. She inhaled sharply and felt his breath, expelled in surprise, caress her ear.

He thrust her away from him abruptly, yet kept his hands clamped on her, making sure she'd regained her balance. His mouth was severe and his eyes unreadable.

"Are you all right?" he demanded.

"I...think," she managed to say. The fear of falling still hammered in her blood, and the stern set of his dark brows made her feel somehow guilty.

"Be more careful," he said, his hands dropping from her. He turned his back and began to walk the ledge with his eerily quiet tread.

Laura sucked in another deep breath. She inched after him, her step not nearly as assured as his. She glanced down, and the incline of the ravine unnerved her. She could have gone crashing down for a hundred feet or more before sliding to a stop.

Did Jarod really think Tim had navigated this ledge? Tim still dragged his left foot when he was tired, and his left arm was weaker than it should be. It might not hold him if, stumbling, he tried to catch at something.

Had he fallen? The thought frightened her so much she was nearly ill. She gritted her teeth and kept edging along the shelf of stone. She did not let herself look down again.

Her heart sank when she saw a second shelf of limestone looming before them. It jutted higher than the first, forming a sort of roof. She had to bend to make her way beneath it.

Jarod moved in a half crouch. Suddenly he turned and held out his hand to her again. Surprised, not understanding, she trusted him and gave him her hand. Once more, his touch sent a bolt of pure awareness through her. But his nostrils flared, and the look he trained on her face was so harsh she could only take it for dislike.

Why does he look at me like that? she wondered, half angry, half dismayed. *Does he really resent me that much? Does he think I'm that much of a burden?*

Then she saw why he'd reached for her, and her dismay turned to anxiety. The ledge narrowed to only a few inches in width.

Beneath them, the face of the ravine dropped away; it was as if they stood at the edge of a cliff.

"He couldn't have gone this way. He couldn't," Laura said, looking into Jarod's implacable gray eyes.

"He did." Jarod's tone brooked no argument. "Now, do exactly what I do. Step where I step."

He gripped her hand more tightly, then made a short series of movements that seemed to Laura as complicated as a foreign dance. He drew her after him, and when she faltered, he leaned toward her, seized her beneath the arms and swung her to safer ground.

Then she was beside him, and they were both breathing hard. The shelf had widened, and once more they were relatively safe.

Laura glanced back in wonder at the section of ledge they had crossed. For a yard and a half it had narrowed to only a few inches. Then, for a space of two feet, it simply disappeared.

How had he maneuvered it? Had he walked on air? Did he have some unfailing gyroscope built into his system—or magical powers? She felt reluctant awe.

He'd released her the second she could stand, as if he found touching her repugnant. He didn't look at her. "Come on," he said brusquely, taking the lead again. The shelf veered sharply to the left.

Laura kept her head ducked because of the overhang. She stepped around the turn, then looked down in fresh despair.

The ledge was about to narrow again; a mountain goat couldn't navigate it, she was certain. She swallowed hard. She wondered if Jarod intended to levitate in earnest this time.

She was surprised to find him staring down at her, an odd expression on his face. "Here," he said, as if that single word explained everything.

His eyes seemed precisely the same gray as the wintry sky behind him, and they held hers.

"What?" she asked, her heart hammering.

"He stayed here," he said. He seemed half pleased, half disturbed. He cocked his head toward the vine-cloaked wall at her back.

Laura blinked in surprise. There was a narrow fissure, almost four feet high yet barely visible. It must be the entrance to a small cave. She would have passed without seeing it, it was so blocked by vines and brush.

"A cave?" she said, still not quite believing it. "He stayed in a cave? But... we're not that far from home. It's only taken us what—four hours?"

He nodded. "He was here. See how the lichen's scraped from the rock?"

She peered at the ledge. It was speckled with pale green lichen, but she could see no sign that Tim had been there.

Jarod pulled back a dead vine that hung across the cave's narrow mouth. "Take a look."

How can he be so sure? she wondered, thinking he showed a singular lack of humility. He hadn't even seen if the fissure actually did lead into a cave.

But it did. Stunned, she stared into its dim interior. It was little more than a narrow tunnel in the limestone, only eight or nine feet deep.

Leaves littered its floor. An oddly concave mound of them was heaped in the farthest cranny of the cave. The floor at the cave's center was scraped bare and blackened, as if a tiny fire had burned there. Near the entrance, the floor was damp, the leaves mixed with a thin coat of mud.

Jarod knelt, holding back the vines and staring at the patch of earth. "His boots," he said, touching a spot gently. "They're the kind kids call 'waffle-stompers,' right?"

"Yes." An inexplicable shiver ran up her spine.

"And the brand was David Guard," he said.

Another shudder trilled along her backbone. He was right. She knelt beside him, trying to stay calm. She thought she could make out the faintest impression of a footprint in the mud and flattened leaves.

He drew one finger long the edge of a crushed leaf. "You can see that waffle print, just barely. And the 'DG' molded into the heel."

"*You* can see it," she corrected. "I can't. How can you? You're *sure* he was here?"

"Most people don't really look," he said laconically. "Yes, this is where he stayed the first day. When you were hunting him."

"First *day?*" She frowned in disbelief. "You think he was here—just four hours from home? In broad daylight?"

He nodded. "This trail's four days old at least." He took his flashlight from his belt, switched it on and made his way to the pile of leaves. He rooted out a small scrap of red-and-white paper. He came and knelt beside her again, holding it out to her. "Familiar?"

She bit her lip in a mixture of excitement and hope. The white of the paper was still clean, the red ink still bright. She could make out half a word: "Nutri-"

She touched it almost reverently. It was the first real sign she'd seen of her brother. "It's part of a wrapper," she breathed. "From a granola bar. Nutri-Farm brand."

"He was here, all right," Jarod said, his gaze moving to the gorge outside. "If searchers walked along the ridge on the other side of the ravine, he saw them."

Laura's throat tightened. "*I* walked along that ridge. Are you saying he hid in this cave like...an animal and watched me?"

Jarod nodded. "Maybe. And he slept. He slept there." He nodded toward the pile of leaves. "When he thought it was safe to have a fire, he made it there." He nodded toward the blackened spot on the cave's floor.

His face took on a sternly thoughtful set. "He's good. He's *very good,* considering his injury."

"Good?" Laura demanded. "How can you say that? It's crazy, that's what it is. To go only this far, then spy on us? And why rest? He couldn't be tired—he'd barely started. Oh, what's going *on* in his mind?"

Jarod cast her a critical look. "Let's take a break here. Let me get a feel for what he'd do next. You're getting rattled."

He moved back to the ledge and sat, stretching out his long legs, then crossing them. He shrugged out of his pack, opened it and offered her a piece of jerky.

"I'm not rattled," she objected, refusing the food. But she was grateful for a chance to rest, and she was hungry and thirsty, as well. She took off her own pack and rummaged through it for her supply of candy bars. Jarod's expression was slightly contemptuous when she drew one out.

"Is *that* what you brought to eat?" he asked, cool irony in his voice. But he looked away from her, as if the sight of her was beneath his interest.

"I just have to keep up with you," she answered. "I don't have to eat like you. What do you survive on? Berries and pemmican? A few nice roots? Some tasty tree bark?"

He shrugged and didn't bother to answer. Laura, frustrated by his coldness, his silences, his speaking in riddles when he did speak, felt a surge of her old spirit and had the sudden urge to push him off the ledge.

"Don't waste your energy on anger," he said, as if he'd read her mind. "It'll work against you."

He was staring into the distance, a slight frown crooking one eyebrow.

"I'm upset about my brother," she said defensively. "He's acting very irrational if he did what you said."

Keeping his gaze on the horizon, he bit off a piece of jerky and chewed it meditatively. "No."

"What do you mean, no?" Laura asked. "Would you explain yourself? Are the woods so sacred to you that talk's forbidden?"

He gave her a short eloquent glance that told her he was not amused. "His thinking was clearer than yours. Or at least it was four days ago."

"*Why?*"

"Because, he has to do more than run away. He's got to evade—" he gestured at the opposite ridge "—anybody who comes looking for him."

Laura unscrewed her canteen top, more exasperated than before. "So?"

He turned toward her, the familiar strict control in his face. "You ever look at your brother's books?"

"Of course. I see them every day."

"I mean really look. Ever notice one called *Search And Rescue Survival Training?*"

"No. I never paid any special attention."

"It's put out by the U.S. Air Force."

"And?" she prodded.

He took another bite of jerky. "It's a survival manual. Tells an airman what to do if he's shot down in, say, hostile territory. In hostile territory, he has two problems—surviving and evading."

"Then why didn't he keep moving?"

Jarod shook his head. "When were people looking for him?"

Slowly Laura began to understand. "During the day," she said softly.

"And it's easier to spot something moving than something still. He stayed still in the daytime."

Her heart sank slightly. "And it'd be impossible to see him here. This place is...is..." She groped for the word.

"Camouflaged," he supplied. "It's naturally camouflaged. And if somebody's searching for you, the smart thing is to go where they're least likely to look. That's why he headed for that briar patch first."

Laura nodded ruefully. Tim's actions weren't nearly as irrational as she'd thought. They were all too rational, which, in its way, was even more disturbing.

The memory of what Jarod called the briar patch reminded her she'd torn her jeans across the shin. She hadn't stopped to inspect the damage.

Now she pushed the right leg of her jeans up and examined her leg. She winced. She had a cut that ran clear to the back of her calf. She realized that it stung—badly, in fact. She had been too intent on the journey to take notice before.

"When did you do that to yourself?" Jarod demanded.

"I hardly remember. It was in those brambles."

"Why didn't you say something?"

"It's not that important," she muttered stubbornly. "Let me have the first-aid kit, will you? And keep on talking. Tell me about this evasion business."

He reached into his pack and withdrew the first-aid kit, setting it beside her. He took a clean bandanna from his back pocket, opened his canteen and wet the cloth.

"I'll clean it," he said.

"*I'll* clean it," she argued. The thought of him touching her was unsettling.

"Hold still," he grumbled. "This is deeper than you think. And you've got a thorn in there." He grasped her leg just above the calf and began to wipe the wound.

His hand was brown against her pale flesh, and his touch was firm. She clenched her jaw as he worked the thorn out and winced again when she saw fresh blood well from the puncture.

He held the kerchief over the spot and swore under his breath. "That's deep. It was like digging buckshot out of you."

"Just let me put the antiseptic on," she said, trying to wriggle from his grasp.

"I'll do it," he said with finality. "You're still bleeding. I want to know it's done right. I don't want you getting an infection."

"Your sympathy overwhelms me. You forget that *I'm* the nurse here."

"I don't want you to slow me down."

He kept the handkerchief pressed in place.

"Tell me more about Tim," she said, her jaw clenching again.

"He'll keep moving for a while. When he settles, he'll settle in places like this one—naturally concealed. He'll avoid obvious places, any area near a landmark of any kind. Anything important enough to be marked on those maps of yours, in fact. And he'll want rough terrain, heavy vegetation."

He took the cloth away but kept his grip on her leg. He opened the tube of antiseptic and smoothed it on.

"What else?" she demanded, trying to ignore the sting of the medication. His hand on her leg made her skin tingle wildly, and she tried to ignore that, too.

He put a patch of gauze over the wound and, using his knife, cut off strips of tape to hold it in place. When he was done, he sat back on his heels, looking at her.

Hurriedly she rolled down the leg of her jeans and flexed her calf, testing the bandage.

He nodded at her empty candy-bar wrapper. "You'd better have another one of those. I hope they're healthier than they look."

Reluctantly she took another bar and unwrapped it; she was still hungry, although he seemed ready to move on. The bars were actually from the health-food section in the grocery store and high in vitamins. She didn't know why he was so critical.

"What else will he do?" she asked.

He trained his gaze across the ravine again. "He should stay someplace high when he stops. Like this. Noise made up high dissipates. And the wind on a slope is less."

He took off his hat and ran his hand over his brown-gold hair. He narrowed his eyes thoughtfully. "He'll avoid main waterways. He'll keep a low profile, leave as few traces as he can. He'll rest—that's important. And he'll move at dawn and dusk. You and I don't have that luxury. We've got to keep after him."

Laura finished the last of her bar, took a final sip of water, then recapped her canteen. "Right," she said. "Let's get going." She knelt and started to shoulder her way into her backpack.

"No." She was surprised when he reached for her pack, his hand closing over its aluminum frame. He took it from her, his wrist brushing hers. He almost flinched at the contact.

She gazed up into his face. His eyes had that shadowed, uneasy look that so worried her. "What's going on?"

"You'll see," he said.

"Jarod, is there something you're not telling me?" she asked. "About what you've seen here? About what he's doing?"

He shook his head and jammed the broad-brimmed hat on, drawing it low over his eyes. He picked up his own pack and started to rise, but she clasped him by the arm to hold him a moment longer.

His body tensed and he stared down at her hand.

She knew she shouldn't have touched him; he didn't like it, but it was the only way she knew to keep his attention.

"Tell me," she said more intently. "I want to know. I'm his sister. I have the right. Something's bothering you about this."

He was silent for some time. He met her eyes briefly, then flicked his glance down at the fire spot.

"*That* bothers me. He shouldn't have resorted to fire yet. It's been cold, but not that cold. It shows questionable judgment. Also, he's left signs of himself here. He's not as careful as he thinks. And this place doesn't have enough escape options. If he makes small mistakes at the beginning, he'll make bigger ones as he goes on. We have to hope he doesn't make one that gets him hurt.''

"That's everything? You're not holding anything back?''

He looked at her hand again, and moved his arm away. "That's everything. Come on.''

She came to his side, and they paused, half-crouched, beneath the overhang. "Which way now?'' she asked, perplexed.

Below the ledge the land was too steep to climb, and the ledge itself grew so narrow that progress along it was impossible.

"Only one choice,'' he muttered. "Up.''

She felt sick at the news. To go up, a man would have to hoist himself to the higher ledge and somehow clamber over it. And who knew if the terrain was any better from the second ledge? It could not be seen.

"Up?'' she asked.

"Up.''

"You don't know what's there,'' she objected. "We could get stuck.''

"I don't know,'' he said. "But your brother did, I'll bet.''

He examined the upper ledge a moment, measuring its distance. He tossed his pack up. Laura heard the *thunk* the aluminum frame made when hit the stone.

He seemed to gather his energy, made a small leap and caught the edge of the overhang. He grimaced slightly as he pulled himself up, and Laura could see the strain in his shoulders.

Then he made some sort of lunge, twisted around and was sitting on the shelf of rock above her. He made it look as simple as climbing out of a swimming pool. He hadn't even knocked his hat askew.

He swung his legs up, then disappeared from her sight. When he didn't reappear, she wondered if he meant her to follow his example.

"Jarod," Laura called nervously, "I don't think I can do that."

He came back to the shelf edge, his face grim as if in disapproval. He knelt, stretching out his arms.

"Hand me your pack."

"I really don't think—"

"Hand me your pack."

She sighed and handed it up to him. She had a sensation of vertigo when she did so. She had to lean farther back than felt safe.

"Give me your hands, both hands."

"But—"

"Do you want to argue or find your brother?"

She blew a red curl out of her eye, set her jaw in exasperation, then reached up to him. He seized her, none too gently, by the forearms.

"Grab my arms. Don't let go."

Laura clutched at him, but when she felt her boots leave the ground, her left hand lost its grip and she momentarily panicked.

Her legs dangled, kicking helplessly into empty air, while beneath her the ravine yawned treacherously.

"Don't fight me," Jarod ordered from between his teeth.

Laura was not conscious of fighting anything except gravity and terror. She kicked more wildly, trying to find a foothold where none existed.

He swore and wrestled her up high enough so that he could grasp the back of her jacket. Roughly he hoisted her by it until he could wrap his other arm around her and pull her to safety.

He fell back across the rock, pulling her to him with a gasp of exertion. She found herself tumbling unceremoniously against his chest and instinctively she clung to him. His arm coiled around her in an iron grip, making sure she didn't fall.

She lay against him, panting with exhaustion, her heart beating insanely and her blood thudding in her ears. She heard him swear. His breathing was more ragged than hers.

He swore again and held her tighter. "Are you all right?"

She kept her face hidden against his chest. His buttons, the beads on his feather, dug into her face. "Yes."

"Still in one piece?"

"I think so," she panted.

He sat up, pushing back farther from the edge, keeping her firmly in his embrace. Then he put his hands on her shoulders, drew back and stared into her face. "Did I hurt you?"

She shook her head, trying to toss her bangs from her eyes. She could not find words.

"Did I hurt you?" he repeated, sounding angry.

"No..."

"Why did you let go?" he demanded. "Why did you fight me?"

She ran her hand through her hair. "I didn't mean to. I was dangling over a...an abyss, for Pete's sake."

She drew up her knees and hugged them, burying her face against them and trying to control the trembling that overwhelmed her. "I'm sorry," she said, as humiliated as she was shaken. "I could have pulled you over."

"No. There was no danger. It was awkward, that was all. Just awkward. You're not that big. You just kick like hell."

"I panicked. I thrashed like a hooked fish. I'm sorry. I won't do it again. I hate it when I lose control." She hit her thigh with her fist, hard. It hurt, so she did it again.

"Look," he said, his tone impatient, "do you have a problem with heights or something?"

"Yes," she muttered and hit her thigh again. "Sometimes. Heights and narrow places. *Damn it.*" She'd thought she could do anything he asked of her, but she hadn't expected to find herself swinging over a chasm.

"Why didn't you tell me? You should tell me these things."

"I didn't know I'd react like that," she said, still hiding her face. "I just didn't know, all right?"

He made a sound of disgust. "Don't take it so hard," he said gruffly. "Next time I'll put a rope around you. Are you sure you're all right? Laura? Hey, Laura?"

She looked at him in spite of herself. She'd fought her tears down, but supposed her eyes still glistened with them. It was the first time he'd called her by name, and it gave her an odd sensation.

He shrugged and rubbed his shoulder. He picked up his hat and flicked dust from its brim.

"You were game," he said dispassionately. "Gus said you were. He'd kill me if he knew I scared you."

She blinked, taken aback, then frowned in disbelief. "Sixty seconds ago I was hanging over this...this canyon, and you're worried about *Gus?*"

"Gus is...fond of you," he said, flicking another piece of dust from the hat. "I promised him you'd be safe."

"Gus," she repeated in distaste. "Hand me my backpack."

He did. Then he stood and picked up his own. He stared down at her with disconcerting steadiness as she put hers on, but he did not try to help her. He made no motion toward her.

"Gus is a good man," he said tonelessly.

She didn't answer. She stood up and willed her knees to keep from shaking. She stared out at the horizon, ignoring his statement about Gus and fastening the straps of her pack.

"I can't believe Tim climbed this thing," she said tightly. "He could have killed himself."

"He's probably been climbing it since he was ten years old. It's not that hard. Women don't have the same arm muscles, that's all."

"He was taking a terrible chance. What if his arm gave out?"

"It didn't give out. He made it."

She wheeled and glared at him. "Well, why didn't you *say* so? And how are you so sure?"

He glanced down at the lichen-covered rock. "There are signs. Somebody's scrambled around here lately. There's a fresh mark on the edge of the shelf. A scar. Made by metal. I didn't make it. His ax probably."

She couldn't imagine her brother succeeding at such a climb. Her own heartbeat was still too fast from it, her pulses too erratic.

Jarod glanced at the sky, and she followed his gaze. The clouds were darker, moving more swiftly, and the wind had grown keener.

"He made it," he said, narrowing his eyes. "I swear that to you. Come on. The temperature's dropping. We want to get to him before it freezes."

Laura nodded, her chest constricting. Tim's decision to climb the rock seemed a dangerous one. There was no way of knowing if he'd made even more dangerous choices. She looked at Jarod, unable to utter her fears.

He didn't glance at her. "Come on," he said his voice harsh. "If you're all right, prove it. Let's go."

She was puzzled by his sudden shift of mood, but he gave her no time to think about it. He'd already set out to the south again. The slope of the incline was gentler here, and his pace was swift.

She adjusted the straps of her pack and followed him, her head down and her heart still pounding too fast.

Ahead of her, Jarod tried to concentrate on following the faint trail Tim Finch had left four days ago: a broken twig here, a dislodged rock there, an occasional broken branch, the rare footprint not washed away.

He hadn't told Laura all he had learned on the second shelf of limestone. The news was bad. The kid had made it up the ledge, all right. But he'd hurt himself. In a crevice of the stone, Jarod had found a frayed strip of cloth. All the rain hadn't been able to wash the blood from it.

Jarod's guess was that the boy had cut himself badly when he'd clambered up the ledge, then he'd torn a strip from his camouflage jacket to stop the bleeding.

And Jarod had seen something else ominous. Whether from the wound or from time in the cramped cave, the kid was limping now.

The signs were undisputable. Even four days ago, the boy was weakening. He wouldn't tell Laura. She was worried enough.

Jarod was worried, too. Tim Finlay'd had half a week to get himself into even worse trouble, and now a freeze was coming, a bad one.

He had to find the kid fast. Not just for the boy's sake. He had to do it for Gus. The sooner he got Laura back to Gus, the better.

She's his, Jarod's mind kept hissing at him. He had to remember that. It was why Gus had brought him here. To help win Laura back.

Jarod had no business thinking of her, watching her and liking too much what he saw. He steeled himself to ignore her.

He led her on, deeper into the heart of the wilderness.

CHAPTER FOUR

IN SPITE OF his best intentions, Jarod not only had to notice Laura, but admire her. She kept pace, didn't ask for special treatment and didn't complain. But he remained brusque with her. He didn't know how else to handle her, and it made him edgy.

She'd recovered quickly from her scare. And she was determined, he had to admit. She reminded him of Gus in that. Jarod remembered Gus doggedly fighting the swamp and cracking his wry self-mocking jokes all the way.

Jarod gritted his teeth and pressed on, struggling to focus on tracking the kid. He found Tim's second hiding place late that afternoon. Another cave, this one set low in a slope over a narrow branch of the Spellbound River. Again there was sign of a fire, and this time the kid had been even more careless with his garbage.

Jarod, now that they were stopped, felt something akin to being trapped. There was no way he could not be aware of Laura. She stood pensively studying a handful of crumpled granola-bar wrappers. The set of her mouth was vulnerable and anxious.

"He's going through his food too fast," she said. "And look at this."

She held up a used tea bag. "He left the string and the tag on when he packed. That's not like him. He was always so conscious of every fraction of an ounce he carried." She shook her head sadly.

"What about you?" Jarod asked, hating the worry that clouded her spirited face.

She looked at him as if she didn't understand his question. She'd kept her hat off, and the red-gold tumble of her curls glinted even in the cave's shadowy light. Her hair, he thought, had the live warm gleam of burning embers.

"I mean what about you?" he persisted. "Do you take the tags off tea bags?"

She shrugged one shoulder, looking at the granola-bar wrappers again. "Of course. He's right—by the end of the day you feel every ounce you've packed."

He nodded in grim agreement. Somehow he'd come to figure her for the sort who'd tear the tags from tea bags when she went camping. She was a surprisingly capable backpacker. Gus probably wouldn't appreciate that, but he did.

He turned away from her and studied the cave, perturbed by the signs he read there, perturbed by her.

"Jarod?"

He tensed when she said his name. She had a low, sweet voice, and when she spoke, it was always as if she was establishing some strong connection between them. He wasn't used to that.

She said, "It's not like him to leave all this litter around. It's a bad sign, isn't it?"

It *was* a bad sign, but he didn't want to worry her. He shrugged.

She came to his side. "Jarod?"

He gave her a brief glance, then wished he hadn't. Her alert lively eyes were beseeching, and the look in them almost undid his heart.

"What do you see here?" she begged. "Tell me. Tell me everything. Please. Don't hold anything back. I want to be prepared for...whatever."

He set his jaw. She sounded resolved to face anything; he supposed he should tell her, at least in part, what he saw.

But still he didn't speak. He usually had no trouble dealing with people and could do it well enough. With her, he felt almost like a schoolboy again. To a man who prided himself on self-reliance, it was disturbing.

She shuddered. "I don't like this place," she said. "It gives me a bad feeling. I wish he'd chosen someplace else."

He nodded. Laura, even if she missed subtle signs, had excellent instincts. She'd picked up the vibrations from this place, and she was right; they weren't good.

The cave was filthy. Its crumbling ceiling had strewn the floor with rubble. Animals had denned there, leaving waste and musty scents behind. Even now, gray bats clung to the walls, deep in wintry sleep.

The place was also damp. The walls oozed moisture, water dripped from the ceiling, and the air was dank, fusty, unwholesome.

The cave was even situated wrong. It was too low on the hill's slope, wind whistled through the entrance, and the floor was thick with mud. The mud held tracks. Tim's. He'd been limping markedly, favoring his left leg.

The kid had spent a restless night. He'd paced, he'd eaten most of his meager store of food. He hadn't been able to keep his fire going. His water must have been running low, and the only source was rain or the muddy creek below.

"He didn't pick this place well," Jarod said carefully. "We passed a smaller cave an eighth of a mile back. He should have taken that. Better cover, drier, tighter. With a spring close by."

"A spring? I didn't see any spring," Laura said.

Jarod went to the mouth of the cave and stared out. "It was there. Clean water's important. He's got to keep as clean as possible. His clothes, his cooking gear—everything. A germ's as dangerous as a grizzly."

She followed him and stood by his side again, as if she didn't like being alone. He shifted uncomfortably. He'd spent so much of his life alone he'd seldom thought of needing people.

"We don't have grizzlies down here, thank heaven," she said. "There are black bears, but they should be hibernating. And he shouldn't have to worry about snakes."

"Or moose," Jarod said out of the corner of his mouth.

Laura gave a short disbelieving laugh. She had a nice laugh, low and with a quirky gurgle. It gave him an odd feeling in the pit of his stomach, as if he were falling off some ghostly cliff.

"You have moose in Maine?" she asked. "They're scary?"

He pulled his hat brim lower. "You wouldn't laugh if one attacked you."

She laughed again, anyway. Once more his stomach did its weird, spooky thing. "A moose *attacked* you?"

He found himself half smiling at her, glad to see that she could still laugh. "Yes."

"Well, what did you do?"

"I climbed a tree—fast."

"What did he do?"

"Tried to knock it down—hard."

"And then?"

"I waited for him to go away."

"A moose," she said with wonder. "I've never seen one. Are there lots?"

"Once one walked right into a neighboring town. In broad daylight. He walked into a shoe store."

Laura smiled. "A shoe store?"

He gave her a crooked grin. She was, he saw, one of those women whose true beauty was revealed in her smile. He liked having created that smile, wanted to keep it there. He told her the punch line of the anecdote. "The owner said, 'He must have heard we can fit anybody.'"

He was rewarded with another laugh. "What happened?"

He wrenched himself back to business. His smile faded. "They had to be careful not to spook him. An animal that big could go through a plate-glass window, hurt itself."

"It's hard to think of anything hurting a moose."

"Man can. And man-made things."

"You're like my brother. A lot. You really love all this, don't you?" She gestured at the woods, the stream winding in the valley below them.

His face grew more stolid. He did not use words such as love.

"Jarod?"

His only answer was a brief sideways glance. Her eyes had turned serious again, and she was studying him with disconcerting steadiness.

"How did you get . . . like this?" she asked. "Able to do this, I mean. Did someone teach you?"

He studied the cloud-riddled sky, which promised greater coldness. "Yeah," he said, remembering. "Somebody taught me."

"Who? Your father?"

His upper lip took on a slightly bitter crook. "No. My father was a bartender. Until he got a little too involved in his work. He started bringing it home."

"Oh," she said, as if she understood.

He shrugged. His father had never drunk on the job, had never been mean when he did drink; he just stayed in a forgetful haze. Among the things he'd seemed to forget was that he had a son. He wasn't an evil man, only a deeply un-happy one.

"Well," Laura said, sounding hesitant but persistent at the same time, "who *did* teach you?"

His expression didn't soften. "A guy. Part white. Part Sioux, part Micmac. He lived on a disability pension. From Korea."

"And he loved the woods?"

Love. That word again. "I guess." In one sense he supposed Raymond Hare had loved the woods. In another Raymond had escaped into them, just as Jarod's own father had escaped into the bottle.

Like Jarod's father, Raymond had a headful of bad memories; he'd been a prisoner of war for two years. He had seen too much of the evil of men, so had sought the peace of the wild.

"Why did he teach you?" Laura asked. "Because you liked it so much?"

He shook his head. "I hung around with his son. I lived as much at their house as mine. He taught us both. Hell, my father probably didn't even know I was gone."

"What about your mother?"

Why was he talking so much? he wondered. How could she make it seem almost easy, almost natural to talk of such private things?

He gave her a glance he intended to be cold, to stop her from asking so many questions. But her brow was creased with concern, and she seemed determined not to be put off by him.

Worse, she gave him the sense that she wasn't nosy, but that she was sincerely trying to understand him. He never encouraged that sort of interest; it unsettled him. Yet with her, it was different.

"I don't mean to pry," she said, "or to raise a painful subject. I— Our mother died. When Tim was five. I know how hard it is. I really do. Did you lose yours, too?"

The line of his mouth grew harder. "She lost us," he said, not sure why he told her.

Laura stared at him in disbelief. "She . . . left you?"

He looked away, studying the cold sky again. "She ran off with a guy with more money. My father's best friend, in fact. He took her to Bangor."

"She left you?" she repeated, clearly horrified. "Wouldn't your father let her take you—"

"She left him. She left me. She never looked back. I haven't seen her since."

"How old were you?"

"Nine." He'd lost patience with himself. He was jabbering like a damned magpie. He was annoyed that Laura could make him do it. "And I don't like being interrogated, okay?"

"I'm sorry. I just find you so—interesting. But—you and your friend—did you both become trackers? Do you work together?"

He set his jaw, because she'd really hit a nerve this time, a raw one. He and Raymond, Jr. had talked about working together, all right. Back then, they thought their friendship would last forever.

He and Raymond Jr. would start their own business running a wilderness camp—they'd be hunters, guides, trackers. They'd had big plans. But none of it had happened.

"He tends bar the same place my father used to," he said shortly.

"So only you carry on your old friend's tradition, his learning. . . ."

Jarod's shoulders moved restlessly, irritably. "No more questions," he muttered, knowing he was being rude. He couldn't help it.

Young Raymond Hare, Jr., had been like a brother to him. They'd even cut their fingers once, pressing the cuts together so that their blood mingled, became one blood. That was when they were children.

But when they were nineteen, Jarod had fallen in love with a girl in a neighboring town. She'd just moved there, a schoolteacher's eighteen-year-old daughter.

Her name was Wendy, and Jarod thought she was the most beautiful, extraordinary creature he'd ever seen. The first time he saw her, it was as if he took an arrow through his heart.

She'd had hair as blond as flax and eyes as blue as a bluejay's feather. He'd been so stricken with love for her he could not even bring himself to speak to her. He'd sent Raymond, Jr., who did not have a shy bone in his body, to plead his case.

He supposed the ending should have been predictable, even to someone as young and naive as himself. Raymond fell in love with her, Raymond charmed her, Raymond married her.

But Wendy wanted a regular home like regular people. So Raymond got an ordinary job with set hours and steady pay. Now he and Wendy had been married ten years.

Sometime during those ten years, Jarod had fallen out of love with her. She no longer seemed extraordinary. She no longer seemed desirable or even especially beautiful. There'd been other women, of course. He'd let them get physically close, but not emotionally. If they demanded more, he sent them on their way. He kept things simple.

As the years passed, he'd more or less forgiven Raymond, Jr., as well. But his friend had changed, and things were not the same between them. They never would be, and both men knew it.

"I'm sorry," he said gruffly, trying to be honest with Laura. "I'm not much of a talker, all right? I don't get personal with people."

She looked abashed, but in a moment her chin was up again. "Sure," she said. "However you want it. I'm sorry, too. I didn't mean to—"

"Let's go," he interrupted, his tone no softer.

"Good," she said. She, too, seemed to become strictly business again. "I don't want to stay here."

She cast a distrustful look back into the cave. "His staying here—do you think it shows his judgment was slipping, or his strength?"

He didn't want to say. The signs the kid had left behind showed he was failing fast.

"He was still going," Jarod said vaguely. "That's what counts."

"And?" she asked, pressing for more information.

He thought of what he could tell her without alarming her. "He'll have to scavenge for food soon. He may hole up in one place. If he does, it's good. We'll find him sooner than if he stays on the move."

"It'll be dark soon," she mused, scanning the sky. "And it's cold, really cold. I wonder if he's moving now? If he's hungry? Cold. Tired..."

Jarod tried to sound neutral again, neither friendly or unfriendly. "Let's go while we've got light. I want to check out the opposite bank. I thought I saw vapor rising. There might be a hot spring."

"A hot spring," Laura said wistfully.

"This state's full of them, right?" Jarod shouldered his pack.

She nodded. They started off, and he set his usual quick pace.

Laura stayed almost even with him. She, too, seemed to be making an effort to turn the conversation impersonal again. "The really famous hot springs are in, well, Hot Springs. That's why the town was built. But there are others here and there."

The descent to the stream was easy, but it was swollen by rain. The water churned, high, muddy and swift. In spite of the turbulence, a ragged skin of ice was forming at its banks.

Light was fading fast. Jarod hadn't been watching for tracks—somehow Laura's questions had rattled him, set him badly off his stride.

Now he had a sudden eerie impression that Tim had come this way. Why? Had he, too, been drawn by the hot spring?

Jarod paced the muddy bank, Laura behind him. He now saw faint but sure signs that Tim, too, had been here—the dislodged pebble, the snapped twig, the trodden leaf.

Jarod followed the dim trail until he came to a tree that had fallen across the creek. It slanted sharply down toward the water, then was caught on an outcropping of stone that jutted into the stream from the opposite bank. Both the log and the stone were wet from the high water.

He eyed the way critically. It was a tricky walk, but the quickest path. It was the most direct course for the kid to take.

He glanced up the opposite bank again. He had a second sudden eerie intuition: there might well be a cave where he had seen the vapor, maybe a cave that kept a constant temperature.

Perhaps Tim had been trying to make his way there originally, but somehow ended up in the wrong place, the cave they'd just left. It made sense: the kid knew the wilderness, but he was disoriented.

Signs of his trail ended at the log. The boy had used the log and stone ridge to get to the other side, Jarod was certain. They'd follow. He wished the kid had picked an easier spot to cross and wondered if the boy'd gotten himself in trouble here. It could be a dangerous place. He decided not to say anything yet to Laura about Tim's coming this way. She was worried enough.

"We'll go over here," he said, nodding at the fallen log, the wet limestone ridge. "I can get across. The question is, can you?"

She swallowed. "It looks slippery."

"It is. Don't try anything fancy. Don't worry about looking dignified. Just get across. Let me go first. Step where I step. I'll hang on to you. If you slip, I've got you."

She bit her lip, look uneasy, but nodded.

He stepped on the tree trunk, testing its strength, its slipperiness. Instinct told him where he should step and how.

He reached toward Laura, offering her his hand. Her fingers were tense, so he locked his tightly around them. Even as he did so, he regretted the action.

For a moment his concentration vanished. He forgot about the valley, the swiftly flowing stream, the sharpness of the cold air. For an instant all his awareness seemed to rush to his hand, where touch joined him to her.

He came back to himself with a jolt, startled. He tried to wrestle down his sexual awareness of her.

"Come on," he ordered more harshly than he'd intended. He wished he wasn't touching her. Her fingers seemed to burn his, even through their gloves.

He started across, taking short quick steps. He would have to make a small leap to reach the ridge of limestone, and it would be tricky, because the ledge was wet.

Laura, he realized, wasn't moving fast enough to keep up with him. Her arm was stretched out full-length and so was his. He tried to draw her after him, make her stay closer.

"Don't," she warned, her face a pale oval in the failing light.

"Don't freeze on me," he ordered, pulling her after him. "Keep close or I'll lose you. Now stay with me—there's a jump, just a little one."

"No," she protested again, but she increased her pace, moving down the log swiftly as he had done.

"Better," he said, then focused on where the stone ridge rose above the swirling water. "Okay, now, hang on."

"No!" she half gasped, but he leapt and landed on the narrow rock as neatly as a cat. He moved most surely when he moved swiftly, but she was hesitating.

His hand tightened on hers. Once more he drew her, resisting, after him. He did not bother being gentle.

"No!" she repeated, even as she tried to make the small jump.

Somehow she missed. Her feet hit the rock where it was submerged, and her legs buckled. She whirled, trying to keep her balance, but fell backward with a splash that spattered the air with icy spray. Her backpack struck the rock. She kept her head and shoulders above water, but the fast-flowing water swept around her, threatening to suck her under.

He almost lost his balance, fighting to keep hold of her. She was amazingly quick, though, and managed to scramble to the rock, bedraggled, on her hands and knees.

He tried to help her, to raise her to a standing position, but she struck at him with force and anger.

"Stop!" she cried, when he didn't let go. "You yanked me off balance. Get away!"

She punched at his arm with such vehemence that he let go. Her words amazed him, flooded him with sudden self-doubt.

"Out of my way. Out!" she raged, splashing toward the shore on her hands and knees. He tried to help her, but she was already clambering inelegantly to safety.

She collapsed facedown on the bank, dripping, her pack sodden, one buckle ripped loose. "Damn!" She hammered her fist impotently against the ground.

He reached the shore, his adrenaline rushing sickeningly. He bent over her, hauling her to her feet. "Laura, are you all right? Can you stand?"

She tried to fight free of him, but sank, struggling against him, only his arms keeping her upright.

"Can you walk? Are you hurt?"

She hit his chest once for good measure, then stared up at him in enraged misery. "I can't stand. I can't walk. My legs are too cold. Oh, where did Gus find you? What kind of i-id-idiot—"

She stopped because her teeth were chattering too hard. Jarod's heart felt as cold as the freezing stream. What had he done to her? Had he really caused her to fall? He never made such careless mistakes, never.

And yet a shadow darkened his confidence. Had he been struggling so hard not to notice her as a woman that he'd stopped noticing her as another human being? Had he blinded himself to her needs, her pace? He couldn't believe he'd been so stupid. He saved people; he'd never endangered anyone in his life.

Yet she had fallen. And now she shuddered against him, unable even to stand.

He cursed himself, he cursed the water, he cursed the world, then he swept her up in his arms.

He pressed his mouth almost savagely against her icy cheek. "Sorry," he said between his teeth.

The cold of her flesh cut through his chest agonizingly, and he held her more tightly still, as if he would let nothing, not even the elements, wrench her away.

CHAPTER FIVE

LAURA SAT in the tiny cave, shivering, mortified and furious.

She wore Jarod's spare flannel shirt, a brown plaid one, Jarod's spare socks, heavy-weight gray, and Jarod's spare jeans, so long she had to roll up the legs halfway. She also wore his parka and felt lost in its folds.

Her own clothing was all soaked, and Jarod, it seemed, eschewed underwear. She would have gladly killed for a dry pair of underpants, whether for male or female.

She huddled before the fire. His unzipped sleeping bag draped around her shoulders like a shawl, and she was drinking a cup of hot cocoa he'd made her from a powdered mix, but she still shivered.

"Look," Jarod said irritably, his brow furrowed, "it was an accident, all right?"

She held her mug of cocoa between both hands and stared stubbornly at the fire. "You *yanked* me off balance."

He frowned harder and threw a stick of wood into the fire. "I thought you were scared again, that you were so afraid to move you'd frozen."

"I'm frozen because of *you,*" she accused. "I was making my way. You told me not to worry how I looked—just to get across. I was taking my time."

He flung another stick to the fire. "It's easier for me if I do it fast, that's all."

"Fine," Laura muttered. "You do the twinkle-toes number. *I* have to take my time. You're supposed to be so observant—couldn't you see? I would have made it at my own pace—but no. Mr. Helpful has to pull me into the Yukon River. What do you do for an encore? Bury me in a glacier?"

The set of his jaw went grim. He kept his eyes narrowed and trained on the flames. "Gus said you had a temper. He said you held a grudge."

"Gus!" She almost spat the word. "Don't talk to me about *Gus*. What a fine pair you must have made—the Two Stooges do the Everglades."

He gave her a look that should have quelled her, but she was too angry. It had been humiliating. He'd helped her strip off her sodden clothing, and she'd been shaking too hard to protest. He'd seen her nearly blue with cold and in her clinging wet bra and panties.

There was a warm spring in the first chamber of the cave—not hot, but at least warm. He'd left the cave and stood outside while she bathed in it. It flowed into a shallow basin that formed a sort of natural tub. Shuddering, she'd sluiced the heated water over her chilled body.

She'd dried herself on the *thing* Jarod carried for a towel. It was clean, but threadbare, with ragged hems. She'd thought of her own soft towel, now sodden with creek water, and mourned its loss.

The bath helped, but it didn't relieve the chill that seemed permanently buried in her bones. She'd been further humiliated when she couldn't even finish dressing herself. She'd had to call Jarod to button her into his shirt and fasten the jeans. Her own hands had trembled too much.

Tremors still shook her. It was his fault, she thought darkly. She *would* have made it if he'd just let her go at her own pace.

True, she had felt shaky with the water flowing so turbulently beneath her, but she would have made it if he hadn't interfered.

Worst of all, the radio was broken and full of water. If they needed to call for a helicopter they were helpless—and it was his fault. Nothing could make up for the loss of the radio. Of all his sins, that was the greatest.

She glowered at him. The cave, at least, was all right. Grudgingly she admitted that, but it wasn't worth being dipped in ice—or the loss of the precious radio.

The entry chamber was clean and tight. It opened to two deeper chambers, and from them, warmer air seeped. Jarod had picked the third chamber for sleeping. The temperature, he estimated, stayed constant, in the midfifties winter and summer. It would have had to have been ninety to warm her.

"You *had* to come here, didn't you?" she asked sarcastically. "Nothing on the other side of the creek was good enough for you."

He sighed and settled his back against the cave wall. The firelight gilded the planes and angles of his face, touched his tousled hair with gold. Shadows hollowed his cheeks, made him look sterner, more ascetic than usual.

He'd made a rough frame of branches and from it hung her clothes, her sleeping bag and her pack. They gave the chamber a damp, acrid smell.

He stared at her across the fire. She shuddered again, whether from cold or from his look, she did not know. She kept forgetting how extraordinary those clear gray eyes were, how beautiful and how implacable.

"Would it improve your mood if you knew your brother stayed here?" he asked, his mouth crooking down.

She pulled his sleeping bag more tightly around her, staring at him distrustfully. "Tim? Stayed here? You're making that up."

He shook his head, his eyes not leaving hers. The firelight flickered over his face.

Laura gripped her mug of cocoa more tightly. "Why would he stay here? It's so close to the other place—that means he hardly moved at all."

He reached into his pack and drew out two pieces of jerky. He handed her one. When she refused it, his face grew harder, more forbidding.

"Eat," he ordered. "You need protein—three and a half ounces minimum. Not those damned candy bars. I've got powdered food I can make, too, unless you're too good to eat it."

Reluctantly Laura took the jerky, realizing she was not merely hungry, she was ravenous. She bit off a piece, but her rebellious spirit wasn't assuaged.

"Tell me about my brother," she demanded. "Was he really here? Or is this some lie you made up to justify getting to this—this glorified hole in the ground?"

"I don't lie," he said, his gaze steady and forbidding.

"You don't? Your friend does," Laura challenged. "He's an expert at it."

"Sometimes Gus's job is to lie. If you'd think with your head instead of your temper, you'd understand. Yes, your brother was here. Yes, he spent time here. For the same reason we're here. It's a good place."

"A good place," she said contemptuously, although she knew his words were true.

"Think what you want," he muttered. He turned his face away and gazed off into the shadows. His shoulders moved restlessly.

He was silent for so long that Laura couldn't stand it. "All right. Have it your way—he was here. What can you tell? *Why* would he stay? This is still only a day's walk from the house. How *long* did he stay?"

He ran his hand over the unruly waves of his hair. He seemed to travel deeply into his own thoughts. "He was probably looking for this place and got off track. When day came, he could see the vapor here from the other cave, the same as I did. What bothers me is that what happened to you could have happened to him."

She sat up straighter, inched closer to the fire. "He got wet? Why? How? What makes you think that? Did you know he'd come over here when we started this way?"

He shrugged as if the question made him unhappy. "I had feelings that he did."

"Feelings?" she asked dubiously.

"I get...feelings. Hunches. I saw signs. When we got here, I saw the hunch was right. That's all." He went silent again, staring obdurately off into the darkness.

She fumbled through her possessions and pulled out a pair of foil-wrapped candy bars. She hoped they'd stayed dry because her stomach was still growling. She unwrapped one, giving Jarod a resentful look.

"This strong silent act gets on my nerves," she said from between her teeth. "Tell me *everything* you know about my brother. What makes you think he fell?"

He exhaled sharply, blowing his forelock out of his eyes. "There are signs."

"*What* signs?" she demanded. "And is there any more cocoa?"

He reached toward the fire, picked up the pan and re-filled her mug. He took none for himself. "All right," he said, settling against the wall again, grimness in his voice. "The signs. There was a fresh fire scar. Here." He stabbed his finger in the direction of their fire. "You're probably sitting right where he slept."

She stiffened in surprise. "You can tell that? What else?"

He shook his head, as if he didn't like his own knowledge. "He had to dry things out. The marks are there, in the dirt. He dragged in a branch to use. It's over in the corner there."

"How can you tell—"

"I can tell," he said shortly. "He spent a lot of time in his sleeping bag. His boots were wet. He set them there." He nodded at a spot on the floor near the fire.

Then he stared into the fire, as if concentrating on something he could see at its heart. "He was warmer here, safer. There's the spring. When he moved around, he was limping. He's got a blister on his left heel. He ran out of food here. He tried to fish, but he didn't catch anything. He had some nuts, some persimmons. He snared one quail. He burned it when he tried to cook it. He's getting more careless."

Laura looked at him in growing alarm. "You're sure of all that?"

He gave her a look of disgust. "Yes. It's plain. Now are you all right? I'm going to hate to tell Gus about this."

His expression was so full of self-accusation that Laura suddenly felt guilty. It was true her temper was quick to flare, but she seldom stayed angry without an absolutely clear cause.

What had happened on the log was becoming less clear all the time. And Jarod was helping her, was tracking her brother with an expertise that bordered on the eerie.

"Listen, what's your first name, anyway?" she said. "I'm tired of calling you—"

He cut her off. "Call me Jarod. Let's not get personal."

His rebuke almost made her angry again, but they had to work together. She wanted to prove to him that she was mature enough to let bygones be bygones. "All right. Listen, *Jarod,* it seemed to me that I was taking my time on that log, and that you hurried me, pulled me. But to tell the truth, I don't know exactly what happened. Maybe I hesitated. Maybe I was freezing up. I don't know. Accidents happen."

"I don't like mistakes, especially mine."

"I was tired, maybe my judgment—"

"I should have seen you were tired," he said. "I wasn't paying enough attention to you."

Laura looked at him across the flickering fire. He was staring moodily into the shadows again. He had that part right, at least, he certainly didn't pay much attention to her.

Most of the time he acted as if he devoutly wished she wasn't there. Even when he'd half undressed her and she was too cold and shaken to protest, he behaved as if the action almost hurt him. He'd touched her as gingerly as if she were made out glass, not flesh and blood.

She finished her second candy bar, drank the last of her cocoa. "I wish you wouldn't bring Gus up all the time," she said broodily.

"Gus is a good man," Jarod said, his tone as grim as hers.

Laura pulled the sleeping bag more snugly around her shoulders, but continued to shiver. "He lied through his teeth to me. About everything. Did he ever tell you what happened?"

Jarod looked stonily uninterested. "A little."

"Let me tell you," Laura said. She wanted him to know in full how treacherous his friend was, and then maybe he'd stop bringing up Gus's name. "It was over two years ago.

My best friend, Sandy and I, were working in Hot Springs. At her father's printing company.''

Jarod lowered one eyebrow in a frown. "Printing company? I thought you were a nurse.''

"I am,'' she said impatiently. "But I wanted more education. I get ... restless. And I'd never lived in the city. I thought I might like it. I wanted my life to be more ... more meaningful.''

"You don't like being a nurse?''

She sighed. "Back then I worked in a lab all day. I drew blood samples. That was *all* I did. Now I'm on the night shift in intensive care. I don't much like it. I liked the day shift better—in the kids' ward and geriatrics, working more with people, cheering them up. I like that.''

"So change,'' he said with a shrug.

"I can't. I have to be with Tim during the day,'' she said, exasperated by his indifference. "Besides, we're talking about Gus. Gus moved into the building adjoining the printing company. He *said* he was putting in a video studio. He *said* he was going to make commercials and things. He *said* his name was Pablo Flores and he was a Spaniard, born in Barcelona.''

Jarod gave another shrug. "So?''

"So? His name is Gus Raphael, he's Puerto Rican, and he was born in Manhattan.''

"He was working undercover,'' Jarod said with disdain. "He couldn't tell you the truth.''

"Jarod, my point is that he was too *good* at it. I think he enjoyed all those lies. He told me his uncle was a baron. A baron. He'd describe all these things to me—the bullfights, the city at night, the Mediterranean in different kinds of weather, the snow on the Pyrenees, the orange groves of Sagunto—the *taste* of those oranges fresh off the tree.'' She gave a bitter laugh.

"So?" Jarod said with the same maddening lack of concern.

"So he'd never *been* to Barcelona. He'd never been to Europe. He was making it all up. I'd sit there all dreamy-eyed, begging to hear more. I thought he was fascinating. What an idiot I was."

"If you begged for more, weren't you encouraging him? Didn't he have to say something?"

"You don't want to understand," Laura grumbled, crossing her arms. She found remembering Gus Raphael almost as chilling as falling into the creek.

She shook her head in disgust. "He did this every day for a month and a half. He didn't just flirt with me or date me— he paid *court* to me, like he was some sort of Spanish grandee. And why? Because the whole time he was trying to get evidence to put my best friend's father in jail. A man I liked. Who was kind to me. Who was like one of my own family. I was living in his very *house,* eating the food from his table, taking his money for my salary."

Jarod's eyes flicked up to meet hers in his unnervingly steady stare. "Did he deserve to go to jail?"

"That's not the point, either," Laura said angrily. "Gus wasn't setting up a video studio. He was electronically eavesdropping on Sandy's father. He was nothing but a high-tech spy. And when he wasn't spying, he was wheedling information about Sandy's family out of *me,* pumping me, and he did a great job of it, too—while I was living under their roof."

Jarod's expression didn't change. "Did her father deserve to go to jail?" he repeated.

"Maybe he did," she said with a rebellious toss of her head. "He had a contract to print tickets for the Superbowl. He was printing extras—a lot of them. Somehow the

FBI got a . . . a *tip.* Big money was at stake. Some of those tickets get scalped for a thousand dollars apiece.''

Jarod's eyes narrowed. "Big money is an understatement. You're talking a couple of million here. How many years did your friend's father get?''

Laura hugged herself against an expectedly hard shudder. Tears threatened to well up and spill over, but she fought them back. "He didn't get any years. He died before the trial ended. A heart attack. He lived just long enough to be humiliated and heartbroken and ruined. The family lost everything—*everything.* The company. The house they'd had for thirty years. Sandy's mother's never been the same. She had a stroke. It's terrible.''

She stared into the fire. Jarod said nothing. Laura shook her head and ran her hand through her hair. "Sandy's never forgiven me," she said sadly. "She hasn't spoken to me since it happened. None of her family has. I don't blame them. I . . . talked too much. I answered too many questions. I betrayed them. They'll never understand that I betrayed myself, too.''

She gave a helpless glance upward. "Sometimes, since my father died and Tim got hurt, I wonder if my family's being punished for what I did to Sandy's. Since Tim ran away, I've been thinking—is this so I can understand how much I made other people suffer?''

"You can't think that way," Jarod said sternly.

"Oh, I know," she said, impatient with herself now. "It's not healthy. It's counterproductive. But sometimes . . .''

Jarod's mouth took on a troubled sideways pull. "Laura, the man was guilty of a crime. If his family suffered, it's his fault. Gus had a job—''

"Stop it," she said savagely, "just stop. You sound just like him. He had a *job* to do. Well, I don't like the way he did it—with such relish. And I'll never forgive him.''

"Even if he gets your brother back for you safe and sound?"

She met his eyes across the fire. "You're the one who'll get my brother back."

"I wouldn't be here if it wasn't for Gus," he said.

We wouldn't be here, she wanted to amend. *You and I wouldn't be alone in the wilderness together.*

She stared unhappily into the fire. "Nothing can make me think I love him again. It was all an illusion. I was a fool. Such a fool."

"Is that what bothers you? That you were a fool? Maybe it's yourself you can't forgive."

She blinked hard because what he said was painfully close to the truth. But he couldn't understand, not really. She gritted her teeth and tried to explain.

"All my life," she said haltingly, as if admitting a shameful secret, "I wanted somebody...special. Not like other men. I couldn't really picture him. But I'd dream about him and think, I'll find you someday. I *will* find you."

She swallowed hard. "I didn't imagine his face or anything like that. But I knew he'd be strong and brave and have this wonderful integrity. This extraordinary sense of honor—like my father. Then Gus came along. He dazzled me. What hurt most was finding out how he lied and lied. And how eager I was to believe. And how stupid."

"He's a good man," Jarod said almost angrily. "He's brave, he's strong, he's got honor. He...cares for you. Why do you have to be so damn unforgiving?"

"Oh," she said in disgust, "what does it take to make you understand? I'm trying to be honest. You won't listen."

"No. You don't listen."

She could not bear to say anything else, so she looked away.

An uncomfortable silence fell between them. The only sound was the crackle of the fire.

At last Jarod spoke, his voice cold, businesslike. "If you need more to eat, take it. If you don't, go to sleep. We've got to start early."

She had his sleeping bag, so she looked at him questioningly.

"It's yours," he said, as if understanding her thought. He said it with as much detachment as a man giving a quarter to a panhandler.

"What about you?" she asked.

He shrugged. "I'll sleep here."

"But..."

"I've had it worse than this, believe me." He closed his eyes and settled resolutely against the stone wall.

"Don't you want your coat?"

He ignored her question, kept his eyes closed. "Go to sleep. Take off those clothes. Your body heat'll keep you warm in the sleeping bag."

Laura looked at him in perplexity. In the firelight, he looked like a man carved of bronze. He managed to give off an unfriendly aura even as he drifted toward sleep. She helped herself to another piece of his jerky, washed it down with a drink from her canteen, then zipped the sleeping bag back into its cocoon shape and settled into it. She pillowed her head on her arm and closed her eyes.

But sleep would not come. She shouldn't have spoken so frankly to Jarod. He hated personal revelations, she knew. But that was minor, for she had more serious worries. Fears about Tim haunted her, and she could not keep her eyes shut.

She lay bundled in the bag's depths, watching the fire throw lights on the cave's low ceiling. Her drying clothes and sleeping bag gave off an odor of muddy river water and toasting cloth.

The chill from the stream still tingled in her marrow, and she wondered miserably if she'd ever be warm again. From time to time, she shuddered, an uncontrollable spasm.

Worse, the longer she lay there, the more she thought of her brother. If Jarod was right, then Tim, too, had plunged into the stream. How cold and wretched he must have been!

If Tim had soaked his pack, as she had, he must have sat in this cave, naked and shivering, trying to warm himself by the fire while his clothes dried. Even his sleeping bag would have been soaked and cold.

And Jarod said Tim was running out of food. That his foot was blistered. That he was limping. That he was growing more careless, more confused.

Oh, heavens, she thought in despair. She couldn't stop seeing the image of her brother, wet and half-frozen, crouched by the fire.

Tim wasn't as lucky as she. Jarod had given her dry clothing, had rubbed her shivering shoulders, made sure she was fed, given her his sleeping bag. And she was well and whole, not like Tim, who was still fighting the effects of his accident.

He could be suffering from hypothermia. At this very moment he could be lying some place, feverish and struggling for breath, with no food or medicine or comfort of any kind. The night was freezing, and he was so terribly alone and so terribly vulnerable.

She began to shake uncontrollably. She didn't know if it was with cold or her fears for Tim or both. But she shuddered, huge, body-racking shakes, and her teeth started to chatter.

Oh, Tim, Tim, she thought, agonized. *Did you go through this? Was it even worse for you? If we find you, we don't even have the radio to call for help—what will we do?*

She didn't realize that Jarod was kneeling above her until he unzipped the sleeping bag. "Wh-what?" she managed to quaver.

"Come here," he said, unfastening her parka.

"What are you d-doing?"

"Warming you. You're worse off than I thought. Here, take off the coat."

When she'd struggled out of it, he slid into the sleeping bag beside her and zipped it shut with one economical movement. He took her into his arms, and with a shock, she realized he'd opened his shirtfront.

"Take off your clothes like I told you to, then put your arms around me," he ordered. "Under my shirt."

She started to protest, but his body seemed warmer and more life-giving than any fire. Awkwardly she began unbuttoning her shirt.

"Put your arms around me," he repeated. "My God, you're still like ice. Why didn't you say so?"

She didn't want to obey, but could not resist. He'd shrugged out of his own shirt, and his skin was smooth, hard and vital with heat. Shyly, hesitantly, she wrapped her arms around him.

His hand twined in the curls at the nape of her neck as he guided her face to his bare chest. He unzipped her jeans and slipped them over her hips and past her ankles.

He undid his own jeans and somehow kicked out of them. His lean legs twined about hers, sharing his strength and his warmth. She closed her eyes. It seemed as if the sun had miraculously turned human and held her.

"Oh," she breathed, pressing her face more firmly against his warm chest. "You feel like a sun god."

His beaded necklace brushed her hair as he hugged her more tightly. "Look," he said, his voice husky and strained, "this is just survival stuff, all right?"

"Survival stuff," she repeated unthinkingly. She clung to him out of the simple instinct of self-preservation. He could be an unfriendly man, an arrogant and puzzling one, but he could be unexpectedly kind, too, and his body seemed perfect to her touch.

"Your face is like ice," he said, his voice low. "I thought you were better. Are you this cold all over?"

His hands moved boldly over her skin, and they felt like a painless fire stroking her back, caressing her shoulders and waist.

"I...I guess it just never really went away," she said, nuzzling closer against his chest. "And I started thinking about my brother. I can't stop thinking about him. And I'm worried about the radio."

"We'll find him. I promise you. We can make it without the radio—trust me."

She sighed a long shivering sigh. She believed him. She believed if anyone could find Tim it was the man who held her. Warm and naked, he was as elemental as fire. In his silent way he made her feel as if she could depend on him the same way she depended on her heartbeat.

There had been the accident at the creek, but he had seemed atypically distracted. She'd been tired and hesitant about crossing as swiftly as he had. Maybe he was right about that, too; it was her own fault she'd fallen.

"Jarod," she whispered against his chest, "what *is* your first name? I'm sorry I lost my temper."

"Call me Jarod," he said, his breath tickling her ear. "This isn't personal."

Laura shuddered again, and his hands moved over her bare back in a way that seemed highly personal to *her*.

"Maybe I'm not sorry," she said, but she kept her face pressed against his bare muscled warmth. He was delicious to her touch, almost irresistible.

The beads around his neck touched her cheek. "What's your necklace?" she whispered. "Is it like what the Indians call medicine? What does it mean?"

"It means nothing," he said brusquely, his breath riffling her hair. "Except to me. It's...private."

"What is it?" she asked drowsily, nuzzling the deerskin packet. She liked it because it was his, part of the mystery of him.

"Things I picked up here and there. A pebble. A feather. One of old Raymond's medals. It's of no importance. Except to me. Be quiet, damn it."

"Oh, don't be that way," she breathed, nestling more intimately against him. "Just hold me. Hold me."

He drew her even more tightly against him. "Gus wouldn't like this," he complained. "But I can't help it. He's got to understand that."

"Jarod, *stop,*" Laura said, drawing back enough to stare at him in the dancing firelight. His face was only inches from hers, and she realized that in its severe way, it was beautiful.

His hands, which had been caressing her back, went still. "Stop what?"

"Stop talking about Gus."

"Gus is..." he began. But he didn't finish the sentence. He didn't, because she lifted her face closer to his, raising her lips to him.

He paused for a long silent moment. Even in the flicker of flame and shadow, she could see the conflict and reluctance that tautened his expression. His nearness made her ache with tension. Hesitantly she brought her lips even nearer to his.

A trembling second passed. Then his mouth bore down and took hers with an intensity that swept her heart away.

CHAPTER SIX

THERE WAS SOMETHING both unwilling and heedless in his kiss, as if he was torn by what he did. Desire and control warred in his touch.

His mouth woke dizzying yearning in her, a wanting so intense it hurt.

Yet she sensed an iron restraint in him that was a warning: *You're only at the near edge of this frontier. Don't tempt me, don't tempt yourself. Beware.*

Laura gasped softly. His kiss melted the ice that had taken possession of her bones. It filled her with the warmth of life, licked her with the flames of desire.

Her fingers tightened against the hard smooth flesh of his back. This time it was he that gasped, almost soundlessly. His kiss grew more constrained, his lips pressed hard against hers, but not moving. Yet his hands beneath her shirt gripped her more possessively, drew her still closer against him.

Laura's heart leapt painfully at the mixed signals. She understood: he wanted her, he did not want her. Physically she stirred him. But in his mind and heart he did not want her. He seemed repelled by his own hunger, disdainful of hers.

Part of her wanted to kiss him back with such sweet abandon he would be intoxicated by it. He would cast aside his fierce restraint and desire her, simply and completely.

Yet she was rent by conflict. Even as his touch flooded her with heat, she was shaken, reluctant in her own right. Tears of confusion stung her eyes. Jarod didn't like her, so why did his long warm body feel so *right* pressed tightly against hers? Why did his severe, grudging mouth taste so bewitching?

Abruptly he drew his lips away from hers. He was breathing hard. Her own breath seemed caught in her throat, and when she struggled to draw it, it trembled.

"Satisfied?" he hissed. "That's as far as it goes. And that was too far."

Anger and accusation edged his voice. Laura blinked in unhappy surprise. His embrace had loosened, although he still held her. He turned his face from hers and stared up at the cave's dark ceiling. She could see his profile, its stern outline gilded by the firelight.

"What?" she demanded, puzzled and hurt.

"Satisfied?" he repeated, a sneer in his voice. "You got what you asked for. That's all your kind wants. Now sleep."

He withdrew one arm from the sleeping bag, put it behind his head for a pillow and closed his eyes. The touch of his other arm, his hand still against her bare back, had grown impersonal.

Laura was half-sick with sudden fury. "Asked for?"

He turned his face farther away. "You kissed me, I kissed you back. You proved your point. Now sleep."

"I proved *what?*"

His sigh sounded disgusted. "You got me to kiss you back. Big deal."

"But you kissed *me,*" she insisted righteously.

He shrugged, and she felt the movement of his bare chest muscles against her breasts. "You asked for it."

Laura raised herself so that she could glower down at him. He kept his eyes closed, his face impassive. "I didn't ask for anything," she said with spirit. "You're the one who climbed in here, took off your clothes and grabbed me."

He shrugged again. "Why'd you do it? To hurt Gus? Is that it? Are you using me to get to him?"

"*Using* you?" Laura fairly exploded. "And you're bringing up Gus again? Get out of my sleeping bag, you... you dog. Get *out*."

"It's my sleeping bag," he replied. "Be quiet. Sleep."

"Then I'll get out," she countered, struggling to extricate herself.

The arm that held her tightened with a swiftness that cut off her breath.

"If you get out, you'll freeze. If I get out, you'll freeze. So be quiet, behave and sleep."

"Oh!" Laura said in powerless rage. "Behave?"

He said nothing, only gripped her more tightly. She thought of fighting free of his contemptuous embrace. She thought of picking up a rock—a large one—and braining him with it.

But although she could fight ferociously if necessary, she felt too weary, too spent. As for striking him, she knew it for the childish impulse it was. And he was right—without him and the sleeping bag she would freeze. She could already feel herself shivering again.

Resentful, resigned, she sank back next to him and laid her cheek against his bare chest again. How, she wondered tiredly, could a man be so cold and so warm at the same time?

Did he really think she'd kissed him first? What colossal conceit. She remembered his lips lowering to hers with fierce inevitability. She remembered much too vividly.

What else had he said? That she'd *asked* for it? Laura's righteousness retreated a bit, losing force. She *had* raised her mouth to his, as if in invitation. She *had* told him to stop talking about Gus. Had he taken it as a dare to act for himself? Perhaps she *had* asked for it—just slightly.

No! she thought in angry perplexity; even if she had, she wasn't responsible. She'd been cold, miserable with physical and emotional turmoil.

He'd bared his body, taken her into his arms, forced her to touch him—how could she have thought clearly? It was his fault the kiss had happened.

But her lips tingled and, paradoxically, her body felt safe in his arms. Each time she shivered, he seemed to will more of his own warmth into her, to give her, like a magic gift, the heat of life.

She snuggled against him more closely, unable to help herself. Once more she let her arms slip around him, under his shirt, his hard back feeling almost hot beneath her cool hands.

She closed her eyes, trying to shut out the conflict that tormented her. She felt nothing except bitterness toward him, yet she couldn't get close enough to him. It made no sense. None.

Her exhausted thoughts shifted and spun in cruel circles. She must not think of Jarod as a man or even a person, only as a means, a means to find Tim.

Tim. Her mind wrenched back to its familiar fearful path. She'd been so caught up with herself she hadn't thought of her brother for a full five minutes, perhaps longer.

She held on to Jarod more tightly, and she began to pray. She prayed fervently for Tim's safety.

At long last she slept. Even in her dreams she worried and prayed. And all night long, she held on to Jarod.

Once she awoke, thinking he had stroked her hair, nuzzled a kiss against her temple, whispered something to her about love.

But that, of course, was impossible.

JAROD WOKE SHORTLY before dawn. The fire flickered low, about to die into a heap of glowing embers. Twice during the night, he'd risen to refuel it. Twice he'd returned to the sleeping bag to take Laura in his arms again.

Both times she'd stirred restlessly when he'd left her, sighed with something like relief when he'd embraced her again. He'd held her, staring up into the darkness, his cheek against her hair. He'd willed his hands to stay still on her body, not to caress and explore its soft curves.

He'd wanted her so much he sometimes had to bite the inside of his cheek, hard. Violently he'd force his mind and emotions away from her. He slept little. Instead, he held his friend's woman in his arms and desired her.

He'd held her and thought of ten thousand things, most of them bitter. He thought again of them now, in the darkness before morning.

Jarod's father had once had a friend he'd trusted. Michael Cross. Michael Cross had violated the friendship and stolen Jarod's mother, who had been a beautiful woman. Jarod had never forgiven Cross or his mother. He didn't think it possible.

He didn't want to be like Mike Cross, whom he despised. Nor did he want to be like Raymond Hare, Jr., who had sworn so solemnly to speak to Wendy on Jarod's behalf, then taken her for his own. It turned his stomach to think of being the same as they.

And yet . . . he held Laura, he brushed his lips against her hair, he ached with the hunger to possess her.

Disgusted with himself, he rose for the third time to replenish the fire. Once again Laura moved uneasily when he left her. He had the eerie sense that she was trying to reach out to him, to draw him back.

This time he would not return. It was too torturous to hold her and not make love. Her shivers and shudders had almost stopped; she was safe now—from the cold. He fed dry sticks into the fire, watched it flare.

He fumbled in the sleeping bag for his clothes. He dressed, then sat back on his heels and allowed himself to gaze on her face by the flickering light. Golden points danced in her tumble of curly hair. Her lashes cast a shadow on the smoothness of her cheek. Her full lips looked soft, vulnerable, kissable.

No, he told himself savagely and looked away. He ached with desire. But he settled against the cave's wall, crossed his long legs and stared into the fire, instead.

Sometimes he could gaze into a fire until it put him into a semitrance, and in that trance, he could visualize things with extraordinary clarity.

But this time the fire could scarcely lull his turbulent emotions. *Tim Finlay,* he told himself fiercely. Where was Tim? How was he?

He shut his eyes and tried to imagine the boy's condition. He saw nothing. But he had to find the kid as soon as possible. Then Jarod could get him and his troubling sister back to civilization. He himself would go home then, to Maine and the peace of solitude.

But he saw nothing. Only shifting veils of gray mist or cloud, a formless void. He didn't believe the boy was dead. He had a strong feeling, however, he was in trouble, perhaps caught in some twilight area between life and death.

Then he had an image of Laura's beautiful green-brown eyes agleam with tears. He could almost hear her voice. *My brother,* she seemed to say in a phantomlike whisper, *help him.*

Jarod swore and gritted his teeth.

He opened his eyes and found himself staring at Laura. She made a small sound deep in her throat that made his groin harden. She turned slightly in the sleeping bag and flung one arm restlessly toward him. Her hand lay, palm up, and he fought the desire to take it in his own.

She was probably cold again, and probably aching from their long hike, and perhaps she was having a nightmare, as well.

It would be easy, he thought moodily, to say to hell with everything, to take her in his arms again, wake her and warm her with passion, then satisfy her so completely she would not recall that pain or cold even existed.

He imagined himself close beside her, kissing her throat, her smooth shoulders, his mouth moving across the silky curves of her body.

No! he told himself again with even greater ferocity. Abruptly he rose and left her there. He went to the first chamber of the cave, to stand in its mouth and wait for the sun to come up over the mountains.

He could stay near her no longer. He didn't trust himself.

"I TRUST HIM *implicitly,*" said Gus Raphael, rather testily. He drained his coffee, then stared out the window, brooding. The sky was still dark, and only a faint gray light at the horizon's edge hinted at dawn.

Susannah shrugged and wondered why he was so snappish. She picked up the coffeepot and went to him, refilling his mug.

He didn't object, but he gave her only the merest of glances, then turned his attention back to the window.

Susannah had been in bed when she'd first heard him. He'd been making surreptitious clinking noises in the kitchen, the sort of noises men make when they're trying desperately to be quiet.

She'd sighed, knowing she wouldn't go back to sleep. As soon as she awoke each morning, her head filled with thoughts of Tim.

She'd risen, put on her old fuzzy pink robe and her over-size glasses. She'd snuggled her feet into the slippers Tim had given her the Christmas before his accident. They were ridiculous things, huge and brown and shaped to resemble bear's paws, complete with black claws, but she wore them because they somehow made her feel closer to Tim.

She'd cleaned her teeth, brushed her hair but didn't bother to pin it up. Then she'd clumped into the kitchen to see what trouble Gus was up to.

He'd been brewing nasty-looking coffee and burning toast. He was fully dressed in gray slacks, white shirt and a conservative striped silk tie. He was freshly shaven and fragrant with subtle cologne. His gold cuff links flashed in the kitchen's artificial light. He looked worried, distracted.

Susannah had shaken her head in grim amusement. Gus Raphael was the nattiest man she'd ever known. He seemed to have made grooming an art form. She'd felt frumpy beside him in her old robe and bear-paw slippers.

And she was as good as alone in the house with him, even though they were chaperoned. Her aunt Mimi had come to stay with them and was sleeping in Laura's bedroom. Aunt Mimi, however, had been tranquilized halfway to oblivion since Tim had run away.

Mimi was the only other member of their small family, and though she was there for appearance' sake, she might as well have been in Timbuktu, Susannah thought ruefully. For an instant she hated the restrictions of a small community. Mimi was in the house only out of propriety—a young woman like Susannah should not be left alone with a virile man like Gus. Something natural might happen—God forbid.

"What's your problem?" Susannah had asked him, raising one eyebrow. "Are you worried about Laura?"

"Naturally I'm worried about Laura," he'd said. "And Tim, too, of course." He'd sipped his coffee and grimaced.

"I think you're jealous," Susannah had said calmly. "You don't like the idea of her out there, running around with the last of the Mohicans. What's the matter? Don't you trust him?"

Susannah hadn't meant to be cruel. She'd simply said what she'd thought, as she usually did. Although Gus protested that he trusted Jarod, he still reacted like a man whose dentist has just drilled into a nerve.

She studied him now as he stared out into the darkness. He was not a handsome man in any conventional sense of the word. He was taller than Jarod and even leaner, perhaps too lean.

His face at first gave the impression of homeliness, but that was merely an illusion. His features, separately, were extremely attractive. He had hooded dark eyes, an elegantly arched nose and a sensual chiseled mouth.

His mouth and lazy eyes seemed at odds with the spareness of his face. He had high cheekbones with hollows beneath them, and he wore his hair cropped short to disguise the fact it was thinning slightly in front.

His expression could be indolent or mocking or charming or dangerous. His was, all in all, an interesting face, an original face. Susannah understood how Laura could have been infatuated with Gus. He had wooed her with great flare and his own peculiar brand of ironic intensity.

Gus's problem, she'd decided long ago, was that he'd been too glib for his own good. Laura might have forgiven simple, plodding dishonesty practiced for the sake of justice. What she would and could not forgive was Gus's facile, honey-tongued and highly creative dishonesty.

It was a shame, Susannah thought, although she never dared say so to Laura. Gus truly seemed to care for Laura and be repentant about lying to her. And Laura *had* been head over heels for him—once.

Gus still didn't look at Susannah, but he seemed to read her thoughts. "What do you think?" he asked, his voice glum. "If Jarod gets Tim back safe and sound? Do you think she'll forgive me then?"

"I don't know," Susannah said honestly. Both she and Laura were in such emotional tumult over Tim, who knew what the crisis might do to Laura's affections?

"If anybody can find him, *he* can," Gus said. "Jarod's good. I want you to know that."

"I believe you. And I'm grateful. I really am."

"God, I wish I was out there with them."

"I know that, too."

"I mean, that way I could show her how I feel about her. She doesn't trust my words. I can't say I blame her, but how many times can a man say, 'I'm sorry'? How many times can he say, 'I love you,' and she still doesn't believe?"

Gus's Puerto Rican accent had become more noticeable, as it always did when he grew excited. Susannah knew the ways of that accent. Gus had called her, asking about Laura, at least once a week for the past two years. At first she'd been reluctant to talk to him. But she'd come to believe in his sincerity even if Laura didn't. She'd come to enjoy hearing from him—a lot.

"Look," she said a bit gruffly, "why don't you let me make you some civilized coffee, a decent breakfast, and then we can play gin or chess or something?"

Gus turned, giving her a darkly sardonic look. "Your coffee's worse than mine, and you know it. I'm *not* playing chess with you again. I hate being beaten in under ten moves. I really hate it."

"Well, if you'd think ahead, if you weren't so impulsive—"

His mouth took on a disgusted twist. "Pure logic bores me. You know what you have in your *cabeza?*" He tapped his temple emphatically. "You got a computer, not a mind. You should cool it, Susannah. A man lesser than myself might feel threatened. Most men would feel threatened."

Susannah crossed her arms and tried to keep her expression indifferent. She'd always been a star math and science student, and now she taught computer science at the high school in nearby Corinth.

She seldom attracted men she liked. Those drawn to her tended to admire her only for her mind. They were always, alas, what Tim had laughingly called nerds back when he was well.

"Look at you," Gus said, his black eyes flicking up and down her body. "You could be a pretty girl. You've got your sister's eyes."

They happen to be my very own eyes, Susannah wanted to counter, but for some reason she did not. She returned his gaze with one of unwavering steadiness.

"But the glasses . . ." He made a hopeless gesture. "Why don't you wear your contacts?"

"They're too much trouble."

"And what's this with your feet? Like you've got bear paws or something. You think a man would find this attractive?"

Susannah lifted one of her feet and looked at its large bear paw critically. "They're comfortable, and I think they're funny."

"And your hair. You know what? You look nice with your hair down. So why do you always have to skin it back, make it into this . . . this sculpture, instead of hair?"

Susannah's patience cracked. "You're a great one to give tips on attracting and holding the opposite sex, aren't you?"

His expression grew somber, almost sulky. He shrugged as if he didn't mind her gibe. "Hey, I'm giving you a little brotherly advice, that's all."

She turned from him and stared down at her bear paws. She adjusted her glasses to distract her from the fact that she suddenly wanted to cry. "The only brotherly advice I want is from my own brother. I wish he was home. And safe."

"Hey, kid, take it easy. We're both just keyed up." He sounded sincerely contrite.

He stepped behind her. She could feel his nearness. He slipped his arms around her waist, rested his chin on her shoulder. "No offense intended. I want to be your brother, too, someday. Brother-in-law. But in the meantime, we're going to get Tim back. I promise you that."

There was nothing remotely amorous in his friendly well-meaning embrace, but she found herself pulling away from him as if from a dangerous flame. She drew herself up proudly and turned to face him again, fiddling with her glasses as she did so.

"Please," she said primly. "If you want to be family, you should know we're not a huggy-kissy bunch."

"I'm sorry," he said irritably. "I was only trying..." He let the sentence trail off, unfinished.

He looked at her, real pain in his dark eyes. "So what do you think, Miss Bear Paws?" he asked. "Do you think I'll be family—or not?"

"I don't know anything. Except that my brother's in trouble."

He was silent for a long moment. Then he reached and took her hand, a merely sociable gesture. Despite her protests against showing affection, this time she let him.

"Listen," he said with surprising gentleness. "You're going to get your brother back—soon. You've got Jarod tracking him, and I've told you—nobody's better. You know what else?"

She shook her head.

He squeezed her hand. "Your sister's out there, too," Gus said. "You know she won't fail. She won't because she's a woman in a million."

Susannah managed a rueful smile. "I know. I keep wondering where Tim is, where she is—how close. What she's doing..."

"It's hardly daybreak. Let's hope that she's got more sense than we do. That she's asleep."

"They didn't make radio contact last night."

"That radio was a piece of junk. The first law of electronics is whatever can go wrong, will."

Susannah nodded. He released her hand and gave her shoulder a fraternal pat. It filled her with such complicated and unexpected emotions that she looked at him warily.

But he didn't notice her. He was lost in his thoughts of Laura, and there was a desirous light in his eyes. "They're safe," he said. "She's asleep. And having long, sweet dreams of me."

LAURA AWOKE WITH A START. She'd been dreaming that she was marooned on an ice floe. She'd been cast there after being torn from a warm refuge that had somehow seemed dangerous and exciting at the same time.

Jarod, she thought, as her eyes fluttered open. The stronghold she'd dreamed of had been a person—Jarod. He'd lain beside her, held her in his arms.

Now he was gone. That was why the landscape of her dream had turned so cold and bleak. Because he was gone.

We slept together, she thought in confusion.

Nothing had happened—had it? No, nothing. Except one long half-angry kiss that he'd said was her fault and she'd said was his.

They'd exchanged accusations, not words of love. But they'd slept as closely entwined as lovers. She remembered the feel of his warm bare chest against her cheek, the heat of his hands on her body. She remembered the naked skin of his back beneath her fingers.

It had all been too intimate. How could she face him again?

Forget it, argued her logical self. If there had been one ill-fated kiss, it meant nothing. Nothing except that for one brief moment, fatigue and tension had won them over, made them foolish.

She would look him in the eye because she had to. They had a job to do. They had to find her brother. Of what importance were a few fumbling caresses and a halfhearted kiss? None. She and Jarod had business, and it was grimly serious.

She sat up, running her fingers through her hair, then scrambled out of the sleeping bag. The fire was still burning, a small neat flame. That meant Jarod had been there to tend it.

He couldn't be far away. His pack was still there. She reached down to the sleeping bag and picked up his parka. She slipped her arms into its sleeves, then pulled it about her as tightly as she could.

The chamber was not smoky, but it still smelled of drying cloth. Her jacket and sleeping bag, hanging by the fire, were still wet, most of her clothing still damp. She clenched her jaw in displeasure.

The cave's temperature was tolerable, but the outside world, she knew, must be far colder. How could she venture into it with wet clothing? Would Jarod make her stay behind while he went on for Tim alone?

She filled Jarod's little cooking pan with water from her canteen and set it near the fire so that she could make tea. Where was Jarod? Where had he gone?

She made her way through the chambers to the opening of the cave. Jarod stood there, a dark shape silhouetted against the light, staring out at the horizon. She gasped involuntarily.

The world beyond the cave had transformed during the night. It was a dazzling world of white and crystal, of frost and ice.

The ground was rimed thickly with frost, every weed, every stone, every dead leaf of grass thickly furred with it. But it was the trees and shrubs that offered the greatest spectacle. They had turned into miraculous ice sculptures, a fairyland forest of beauty and delicacy.

An ice storm, she thought in wonder. One of those peculiarities of Southern weather that, though dangerous, created a world almost too lovely to look upon.

As the sun rose higher, the ice would sparkle more, filling the air with darts of refracted light. If the day was warm, the ice would melt. The illusion of a fairyland would vanish and the trees would become ordinary trees again.

But if the cold held, then the ice forest would stay, gleaming in both sunshine and starshine, a world etched in silver.

She moved to Jarod's side. He kept staring out at the ice forest, his eyes narrowed against its growing brightness.

"It's beautiful," she breathed.

"It's treacherous," he said without emotion. Then he gave her a sideways glance. For a moment his gray eyes held hers, and her heart seemed to soar higher than the highest ice-kissed branch.

"Treacherous," he repeated.

She nodded, knowing he was right.

But beautiful, too, she thought, her pulses hammering. *Beautiful, too.*

CHAPTER SEVEN

DURING THEIR MEAGER breakfast, Laura and Jarod quarreled furiously. Her jacket and sleeping bag were still wet. He insisted that if she came with him she must wear his parka.

"That," he stated with finality, "or you stay here. I'll leave the sleeping bag for you."

He knew his tone was tyrannical. He didn't care. He must maintain a psychological wall between them.

Laura sat across the fire from him. The thick tumble of her hair shone, glinting sparks, reflecting the flames. He saw sparks in her eyes, too. Lord, he thought, fighting with her was like fighting a whole battalion. He'd never met anybody as stubborn—except Gus.

"I won't stay behind," she argued passionately. "And I won't take your coat."

As if to prove her point, she shucked his coat and threw it at him. It landed, a misshapen heap, in his lap.

He had a stubborn jaw to begin with, and he could feel it jutting more stubbornly now. "I'm used to cold. You're not. In Maine this is practically summer."

"I refuse special treatment. I can put some kind of outfit together. Some of my things are almost dry."

He didn't bother being nice. He sneered. "Don't be lamebrained. I'm in charge. Do as I say. Or you can damn well stay behind."

"You said I botched crossing the creek. Fine. Now I pay the price. I'll wear the sleeping bag, damn it. Like a shawl."

"You said I yanked you into the creek. Fine. I'll pay the price. Put on the coat or I'll do it for you."

At last she gave in. "I'll take your stupid coat," she said with a rebellious toss of her head. "I won't waste any more time or energy over it. Arguing with you is like arguing with a rock."

He tossed the parka back so that it landed in her lap. A look of resentment crossed her face, and he was glad. "Put it on and hurry up. I'm being paid to find your brother—not baby-sit you."

"Paid?" Laura asked, clearly stung. "Gus is paying you to do this?"

"What'd you think? I do it out of the goodness of my heart?"

He was not telling the truth. Gus wanted to pay him, Jarod refused to take anything, and the two of them had yet to settle. But if Laura thought this was only a matter of money to him, all the better, all the safer.

He drained the last of his tea, rinsed out the cup and the pan, then dried and packed them. He pulled his broad-brimmed hat low over his eyes.

He picked up his pack and stood, swinging it into place. "I told you to hurry," he said between his teeth. "This cold isn't doing your brother any good."

She bit her lip, as if to keep from answering sharply. It was a beautiful lip, and he'd like to nibble it himself. Nibble it, kiss it, taste it, possess it—

Mentally he gave himself a swift and savage kick. He forced his face to be stonier than before.

Hurriedly she cleaned her cup and started to pack it, along with a few items and her driest clothing.

"Leave the pack," he muttered. "We can live out of mine."

As he expected, she didn't yield easily.

"Why?" she asked sarcastically. "So I can be totally dependent on you? No, thanks. And I won't have Gus Raphael paying for this. *I'll* do it. We'll have to work out a payment plan, but..."

When her pretty jawline took on that obdurate set, it made him half-crazy with desire. He turned away. "Gus already paid," he lied. "Work it out with him. I've got the money. That's all I care about." He turned his back and headed for the cave entrance.

"Money?" she called after him. "There's a boy out there, a boy's who's not thinking straight and almost certainly in trouble, maybe even..." She couldn't complete the sentence.

Don't be idealistic, don't be moral, he wanted to tell her. *Because that's one of the reasons I like you.*

He paused just long enough to snarl a reply over his shoulder. "To me he's a business proposition. That's all." Then he left her behind.

Laura rose, put on the parka again, then shouldered her pack into position. She snatched up her gloves, which mercifully were dry, strode after him and caught up with him at the cave mouth.

She almost put her hand on his arm to command his attention, but something in his stance was so forbidding that she hesitated. She did not touch him.

"Jarod," she said, "my brother is all I care about. But in the meantime, get this straight— I'll pay your fee, not Gus. You work for me, do you under—"

He cut her off. "I've been paid. I told you—settle with Gus, not me. Now be quiet, will you? I have to concentrate."

Coatless, his back still to her, he set off, striding as confidently as if he had a map that led straight to Tim. He climbed the slope at an angle.

Laura wrestled down the desire to pick up a rock and fling it at him so hard it would knock him over. He'd been so curt, rude and overbearing this morning she wondered how she could possibly have imagined she'd *liked* nestling in his arms, had even been, well, almost excited by it.

She squared her shoulders, cursed him silently and set off to catch up with him.

The hillside was steep, and matching his speed was hard. She ached from yesterday's exertion, and her boots, still damp, were uncomfortable.

When she was nearly even with Jarod, she cast him a suspicious look. "You're hardly looking for a trail. How can you be sure he came this way?"

"I figured it out," he said from between his teeth. "I told you—be quiet. I've got to concentrate."

I can't stand you, you lout, she thought, narrowing her eyes in dislike. *You belong in the woods with the other animals.*

Yet she followed him as if her faith in him was complete. Her pack wasn't heavy because he carried most of the weight, and she wasn't cold because he had given her his coat.

All day long they threaded their way through the ravines. At first they kept to what Jarod called the military crest, a line near the top of the steep that offered both protection and a vantage point.

Shortly after noon he veered downward, tracking some irregular path that only he could see. Laura followed, struggling to keep up with him.

She had stopped speaking to him, because when she did, he answered only in monosyllables. If that was the way he wanted it, fine. Her life would probably be infinitely more pleasant if he never said another word to her.

Overhead the ice-crusted limbs creaked and popped when a breeze stirred. Laura and Jarod's footsteps crunched softly in the frosted weeds. Now and then a redbird gurgled its song or a blue jay shrieked. Jarod's parka was too big for Laura, and its folds whispered as they rubbed together. But as for words, they might as well not exist.

Without words, the world seemed simpler, more immediate to the senses. The ice did not melt, and the wilderness stayed crystalline, almost supernaturally beautiful. And, as Jarod had said when he was still talking, treacherous.

The ground was slippery, rocks icy. When Jarod and Laura were in difficult terrain, he watched her with a closeness that made her skin tingle. She slipped a dozen times or more. Somehow he always managed to catch her; it was as if her tumble into the creek had sensitized him to such dangers.

Each time he caught her, seizing her by the hand or shoulders or waist, the swiftness and sureness of his moves rippled through her like an electric charge. For a split second, the two of them would stare at each other with intense awareness. But the instant she regained her balance, he would release her with a motion that was nearly contemptuous. He would look away, his face grim, the set of his mouth bitter.

The first few times he'd prevented her from falling, she'd muttered a grudging thanks. He'd said nothing, only turned from her and kept heading deeper into the forest. The third time he'd rebuffed her, she'd vowed not to speak again.

In late afternoon, Jarod slowed his pace. He seemed to look more painstakingly for signs of Tim. Laura was grateful, not that Tim's trail had grown fainter, but that she, too, could slow.

Her damp boots chafed her feet. Not once had Jarod taken a level path, and her aching muscles protested the never-ending punishment of the slopes.

By sundown she was struggling not to stumble. Jarod was edging down the side of a ravine that seemed as steep as a cliff. He kept piercing her with his disconcertingly watchful glances. She followed, wondering if he was subjecting her to some cruel test, trying to make her beg him to slow or stop.

But it was he who stopped, abruptly and with no warning. He reached an icy ledge of limestone, paused and looked back at Laura, his face devoid of expression.

Then he disappeared. It was as if the hill's bleak and stony side had swallowed him up.

Laura was too tired to be surprised. All she wanted was to be safely home with Tim. A slightly insane chant had begun to play in her head: *Tim, let's go home now. Tim, Tim, let's go home.*

She reached the ledge where Jarod had disappeared. She wondered vaguely where he had gone, but hardly cared. He might have turned into a hawk and soared away for all she knew.

Tim, let's go home now. Tim, Tim, let's go home.

Then Jarod appeared again, as suddenly as he'd vanished. Silently he stepped from a tall crevice in the hillside. It was as wide as a man and twice as tall.

Oh, she thought wearily, *another cave.* She didn't know whether to be happy or sad. Her feet were numb, and her knees threatened to buckle if she didn't rest. But she did not want to sleep in a cave—or near Jarod. She wanted only to be in her own soft bed, in her own cozy room, with her brother safe, well and snug in the room beside hers.

Jarod looked at her—critically, of course—then nodded, signaling her to join him. He stepped back through the opening. She hesitated, then followed.

Her eyes, accustomed to the ice-whitened world, did not adjust quickly. Yet immediately she sensed that this cave was like the last in one way: its temperature was stable, unaffected by that of the outer world. It was about fifty degrees.

Accidentally she bumped into Jarod. She felt him flinch away as though in distaste. He snapped on a small flashlight, letting the beam play around the interior.

The cave was larger and more angular than the last. From its far wall came a sound somewhere between a drip and a splash.

Water again? she wondered.

Jarod walked silently toward the sound, and Laura trailed behind him, not wanting to be left in the dark. The flashlight's yellow beam played across the rugged back wall of the cave, came to rest on a jut of rock from which a small stream of water oozed, falling to the cave's floor.

The water pooled there in a shallow depression it had worn. As new drops made it overflow, the water wended away in a tiny stream, then disappeared down a crack.

Laura stripped off her glove and put out her hand. A drop fell into her palm, lukewarm—again they had found a heated spring.

Jarod played the beam across the floor. In the cave's farthest corner lay a small pile of garbage, almost covered by a screen of dead brush.

What? she thought in perplexity. The light glinted on the pile of litter: four noodle-soup cans, four cola cans, a tin that had held evaporated milk, one that had held peaches and a dirtied piece of plastic wrap. She moved closer.

Although the outsides of the cans seemed old, their interiors gleamed as if they'd been just opened. They showed no rust, no discoloration, little dirt.

Abruptly Jarod turned the light to sweep the floor once more. In another sheltered corner, Laura saw the familiar fire scar, larger this time. Near it was a small pile of wood that looked old but dry.

"He's been here, hasn't he?" Laura asked, forgetting that she and Jarod weren't speaking.

"He's been here. Not long ago."

Laura was confused. "But...those cans look freshly opened. You said he'd run out of food."

"He had, the fox." Something akin to admiration tinged Jarod's voice. "He fooled us. He had food stashed here. And drink. Even wood."

He bent and picked up a barkless branch. He thrust the flashlight under one arm and dug matches out of the pocket of his jeans. He lit one and held the flame to the branch's tip. Quickly the dried wood took fire.

Jarod switched off the flashlight, thrust it back into his belt. He lit a second branch from the first then handed both to Laura. They were crude torches, but good enough.

Laura held them while Jarod quickly built a larger fire than usual. Soon its light danced on the uneven walls. He looked around the cave's interior with a tight-lipped smile of satisfaction.

Without a word, he took one of the torches from Laura. He knelt, looking closely at the cave's floor. "Oh, yeah," he said with that same restrained satisfaction. "He was here, all right. Still limping. He was tired, maybe damned tired. Maybe even sick. But he wasn't starving. And not down or out. Not by a long shot. I wonder what he had here besides food?"

Laura sat on a stone and unceremoniously shed her pack. She rubbed her aching legs. Any sign of Tim comforted her, but she was too weary to make sense of Jarod's words.

"I... don't understand," she said.

"You will," he replied. "Let's eat. Then get some rest. We want an early start. I think we're right behind him now. Oh, yeah. We've almost got him now."

His words gave her a fresh rush of adrenaline. She stared at him, her weariness almost forgotten. He was still kneeling, this time before the fire, his pack beside him. He set out his cooking utensils, his Spartan food supply: tea, dried soup, protein sticks, dried fruit.

She stared at him across the flames, savoring what he'd said. *We're right behind him now. We've almost got him now.* "Do you really think so?" she asked, almost afraid to hope.

"I know so. We've gained on him."

He began making a simple supper. Laura didn't think to offer to help. Her thoughts were too much on Tim.

"How can we be gaining? We should be at least two days behind him."

"One day," he corrected, filling the two small cooking pans with water.

She frowned, perplexed. "Last night you said we were two days behind."

"We're catching up. From the looks of things, he spent two nights here. Resting. At least he had enough savvy to do that. Probably went on when the food ran out."

"Resting? Two days? How can you tell? The food—I don't understand about the food."

He looked up and gave her half a smile. Her heart seemed to stumble, fall. *Heavens,* she thought. *He's got a beautiful smile. Why doesn't he ever use it?*

"The signs say he was here awhile. As for the food, you said he spent a lot of time out here. Even as a kid."

She nodded, trying to shake off her fascination with his fraction of a smile. *Oh, Jarod,* she thought, *why couldn't you be this human all the time?*

"Well," he said, feeding the fire another small limb, "he played survivalist. He picked the best caves he could find. He cached food." He nodded toward the flames. "Even firewood. Probably in high school."

Laura drew her knees up and clasped her arms around her aching legs. "Is that why those cans look so sorry? They've been sitting in this cave for years?"

"I'd say so. It explains what I found last night."

She cocked her head, intrigued. "What?"

"Look in the pocket of the parka. The lower left one."

She picked up the coat and rummaged in the pocket. She felt something, grasped it, and drew out her hand. She stared down into her palm. She held the rusted cap from a bottle of cola.

"A bottle cap?" she asked, looking at him again.

He nodded. "Found it in a crack in the cave's floor. Too rusty to be recent. My guess is he had a cache there once, but since it was so close to home, he used it for a picnic a couple of years ago. At any rate, even if the food was gone, the place was dry and warm, and it had a water supply."

"He had food here, though," she said with relief. "And even dry wood."

"Right," said Jarod, sounding more optimistic than she'd ever heard him. "My guess is if he cached food in two caves, he cached it in more. So far he's picked good caves—solid shelters, steady temperature, even hot water. The kid practically has himself a chain of hotels out here."

She smiled at the image, but quickly sobered. "But will he know how to get to the next one? He miscalculated the first time—when he spent the night in that dreadful hole. What if he gets confused again? What if he can't find the next cave, the next cache?"

Jarod's half smile fell away. "He *could* get confused. It's possible. Even probable. But we're a lot closer than we were."

She shook her head worriedly. "I don't understand how he even got this far. He's forgotten so much. How can he remember this?"

Jarod looked at her across the flames. "Some things are written here," he said, tapping his temple. "They can be knocked out, erased."

His hand moved to his chest. He tapped again, over his heart. "But some things are written here. Nothing erases them. Not as long as you live."

She wanted to believe him, but couldn't. "That's not always true."

His eyes met hers. "If it's not true, how did he get this far?"

She made a small, helpless gesture. "I...don't know. His injury half destroyed so many things he used to do well—reading, writing. And math. He used to be like Susannah—so good at math."

He filled a metal mug with hot water, put a tea bag into it and handed it to her. "All those things should come back to him—at least in part. It just takes time."

She looked down into the cup and attempted a rueful smile. It failed. "That's what everybody told him—it takes time—but that explanation didn't always help."

"Well, when you get him back, keep telling him, anyway. He's got to understand."

She looked at him again, frankly curious. "You sound like you've been through this. Have you?"

He sighed harshly. "Yeah. A kid in my high-school class. Car wreck, same as your brother. It was like his whole world fell apart. He had to put it back together, but somebody'd stolen half the tools he needed to do it."

"And did he? Put his world back together?"

Jarod lifted one shoulder in an indifferent shrug. "Mostly."

"What's he do now?"

"He's assistant foreman in a shoe factory. A fishing guide on weekends. I'm going to hire him as a guide full time one of these days. He's a good guy. I like him. He knows his stuff."

"You? Hire him? Why? How?"

He stirred dry soup mix into a mug of hot water. He handed it to her. "You ask a lot of questions."

"Yes, I do. Why would you hire him as a guide? Do you work as a guide yourself? Besides doing this?"

His face took on its guarded, noncommunicative expression. "Sometimes."

"And you're thinking of expanding the business?"

"Yes."

"Do you have a lodge or a camp or something?"

"No."

"But you want one?"

The line of his mouth grew grimmer and one brow drew down in half a frown. "Yes."

"Do you think you'll have it? Someday soon, I mean?"

He shrugged again. "Yes. Look, there're protein sticks here, fruit. Eat, don't talk, okay?"

Laura narrowed her eyes at him. "Jarod, why do you *do* this to me?"

He sat back, leaning against the cave wall. He sipped his tea, bit off a piece of jerky stick. "Do what?" he muttered.

"Shut me out. Not talk. You were bad yesterday. You're worse today. Tell me about your friend. About your plans. About yourself. What's your past like? What do you want your future to be like?"

He raised his gaze to meet hers, and as always she felt a quivering shock resonate through her. Although his face showed no emotion, his eyes seemed full of conflicting ones, hypnotically so.

"Did you ask Gus this many questions?" he asked, his voice cold.

Laura stiffened with resentment. "Yes, I did. And he answered with lies."

He swore softly. "You don't just hold a grudge. You squeeze it senseless. You're a minister's daughter. Aren't you supposed to be forgiving?"

She put aside her empty soup mug and sat on the stone holding her tea mug in both hands, her back ramrod straight. "It seems easy for everybody else to forgive Gus," she said, steel in her voice. "You all talk alike. My father said it. Tim said it, too." Her voice grew mocking as she mimicked them. "'The man was doing his job. He really seems to care for you. Give him a chance.' Susannah *thinks* it, but she's smart enough not to say it."

"What if they're right?" Jarod challenged. The firelight licked his face, gave his stern features an oddly tormented look.

"What if they are?" Laura demanded. "Right and wrong don't matter to the human heart. It cares, or it doesn't care. And I don't care anymore. I can't."

His eyes, unwavering, seemed to pierce her. "You did once."

"I cared for a gentleman, a man with...artistic leanings. A worldly man from Barcelona. He wasn't like anybody I'd ever known. Fascinating...and honest, I thought.

But he wasn't real. And he wasn't anything like Gus. So, no. I didn't care for Gus. I...I hate him for what he did."

"People say that hate is the reverse of love. Different sides of the same coin. That coin is deep feeling. So you do care—even if you won't admit it."

"People don't always know what they're talking about," she returned. "Hate may be one side of the coin. But the only thing on the other side is indifference. When the hate finally goes away, that's all that'll be left for Gus—indifference."

"Indifference means feeling nothing," he said. "That's not what you feel."

She sighed in frustration. "My father kept telling me to forgive him. But he didn't understand. He was too good, my father. He helped people. I wanted to be like him, and I wanted to find a man who was like him. But Gus only pretended to help people. He hurt more than he ever helped. Why won't anybody admit that?"

Jarod shook his head. "Justice isn't that simple, Laura. Can't you admit that? His job is to catch lawbreakers. He can't help it if the lawbreakers have family, even innocent family."

"It's not right," she said stubbornly. She met his eyes and held them. "You're not like that. You help people. You never hurt anybody—even accidentally."

He looked away. "It's different."

"No," she said, "it's not."

One of his dark eyebrows rose cynically. "We're going to find your brother. Then you *owe* Gus. You won't feel any gratitude? No spark of warmth?"

"Who knows what I'll feel?" she said, her weariness flooding through her again. She finished her tea, set down the cup and put her elbows on her knees. "But I'll tell you this, Jarod. Whatever I feel, it won't be love. Once something like that dies, it's dead forever.''

"Forever's a long time," he said.

"Yes, it is," she returned, her voice flat with cynicism. She reached for a dried apricot and wondered why Jarod kept staring at her. Was he feeling morally superior to her because she refused to forgive Gus? Was he capable of feeling anything at all? She didn't know.

"What about you?" she said, confronting him. "Didn't you ever imagine you were in love with someone? And later know you were wrong? Or are you above all that?"

The corner of his mouth gave a twitch of distaste. At first she thought he wasn't going to answer. Then the corner of his mouth twitched again, and a small muscle jerked in his jaw. "Once," he said.

"Will you tell me about it?"

"No." He turned his gaze to the flame. "Finish eating. Go to sleep. You can have the sleeping bag."

"That's not fair. I've had your coat all day."

"Take it," he said, acid in his voice. "I don't want to argue about it."

He picked up the used dishes and pans, then rose, heading toward the small dribble of a stream to wash them. He kept his back to her.

"Then at least take your coat," she said, unzipping it. "You can't just sleep on the ground in your shirtsleeves like that. You must have been cold all day."

"Don't worry about it," he muttered. "I've been colder, and I've slept in the damn snow before. This is nothing."

"Oh, you're *so* tough," she mocked. "I bet you can bite diamonds in two."

He shrugged and kept his back to her. His stance said, *I'm ignoring you. I intend to keep ignoring you.*

"Barbarian," she said under her breath. She helped herself to more of his soup, two more dried apricots and finished off with another protein stick.

Then she began unlacing her left boot. Her feet had come back to painful life, and they throbbed. Drat! she thought gloomily. *He'll despise me if I've hurt my feet. That's the first rule of backpacking: never abuse your feet.*

She wrenched the boot off and grimaced. Then she peeled off Jarod's thick gray sock. The top of her foot was chaffed from toe to ankle, and a blister was forming on her heel.

Great, she thought gloomily, and today she'd come to think of her left foot as her *good* foot. She pried off her right boot and winced when she saw a large spot of blood on the heel of that sock and a smaller one on the toe.

She swore mentally and began the painful work of stripping the sock away. Her right foot was more damaged than the left, two spots rubbed to smarting rawness.

She sighed, then reached into Jarod's backpack for the first-aid kit. Trusty moleskin and adhesive, she thought unhappily. She prayed she wouldn't have to ask Jarod to slow up on her account.

His voice interrupted her unpleasant reverie. "What the hell—"

She looked up to see him standing on the other side of the fire staring down at her. His dark brows drew together. "What'd you do to yourself?" he demanded.

"What's it look like?" she asked with spirit. "I've just had a pedicure at Elizabeth Arden's beauty spa."

"Don't be cute."

"I'll be as cute as I please."

He set down the cleaned utensils and came to her side. He knelt and took her right foot in his hand. She tried to jerk it away, but his grip was too sure.

"Why didn't you say something?" he demanded.

"I'm not a wimp," she said. "I wasn't about to complain. You'd enjoy it too much."

He swore softly. "You know something? You've got more pride than sense."

"Thank you very much."

He took an antiseptic wipe from the kit, broke it free of its pack and began to swab her foot.

"I can do that myself," she protested, once more trying to wriggle free of him, but couldn't break his ironlike grasp.

"Yeah? Well, I can do it better."

"I'm a *nurse.*"

"Are you an acrobat, too? You'll have to twist like a pretzel to get to this spot on the side."

"What spot? Ouch!"

"*That* spot. Be quiet."

"Don't tell me to be quiet."

"Be quiet," he repeated with such ferocity she became too angry to speak.

He swabbed both her feet and patched them with badges that he expertly cut from the feltlike moleskin

He was working on the toes of her left foot when she trusted herself to speak again. "Your hands are freezing, Jarod. Have you been that cold all day?"

"That's my problem, isn't it?" he said curtly. "Good grief, why didn't you let on that you were doing this to your feet? Why didn't you at least limp or something?"

"I *was* limping. You didn't notice. Rather, you didn't bother to notice."

For some reason, her words made his shoulders stiffen and his hands go momentarily still. He looked up into her eyes. A small frisson ran up her spine, as if it was being tickled by butterflies.

His gaze held hers for such a long charged moment that she glanced away, nervous. The butterflies had migrated to her stomach.

He finished patching her foot, his touch more gentle than before. But his hand still gripped her ankle, almost possessively. The fickle butterflies flew to where he touched her, sending shivers through her.

His hand lingered, unmoving. She stole a furtive look at him. His head was slightly bowed, and she supposed his eyes were trained on her injured foot.

When he finally spoke, it was from between clenched teeth. "I'm sorry."

She blinked. "You? Sorry?"

He exhaled, an exasperated sound. "Yes. Gus would want me to take better care of you than—"

Impulsively she put her hands on his shoulders. He looked up at her, surprise making his gray eyes warier than usual.

"Jarod," she said, her voice strained, "please don't talk about him anymore. I don't want to hear about him."

He rose so that he knelt on one knee, and his face was even with hers. He still held her bare ankle. His face, usually so impassive, was pained. He glanced at her hand on his shoulder, then back to her face.

"I'd rather hear about you," she said. The words surprised her. So did her voice, which sounded breathy and slightly choked.

His face drew a fraction of an inch nearer hers. "I can't," he said, but he leaned nearer still. "You're his."

"No," she said. The word hurt her, and she clasped his shoulders tighter. "I'm not," she said. "I'm really not."

He exhaled again, a long, soft, shuddering sound. He was so close now that she felt his breath warm and tickling against her lips.

"No," he repeated. His hand left her ankle, rose slowly as if involuntarily and settled on the back of her neck, guiding her face so that his lips hovered only inches from hers.

"No," he said, his other hand sliding under the parka and settling firmly on her waist. "You're not his, are you?"

"No," she said in a small voice almost like a whimper.

She didn't know if he heard her, because he was already pulling her against him, his eyes closing and his lips parting to take hers.

Her own eyes fluttered shut. His mouth upon hers was at first reluctant, restrained. Her own lips answered his hesitantly, trembling slightly.

But then his hunger broke through, igniting hers, and he kissed her until nothing was left in the universe but that burning kiss, forbidden, reckless and heart-shakingly sweet.

CHAPTER EIGHT

JAROD'S ARMS WERE under the parka, crushing her body to his as if he could not draw her near enough.

He kissed her with devouring hunger, his lips making love to hers. That was all she could think: this was no simple kiss—it was lovemaking. The way his mouth moved on hers swept away her resistance. He demanded the innermost essence of her, demanded to possess her completely.

His hands moved voluptuously over the curves and planes of her back. She found herself winding her arms around his neck, slowly, like one mesmerized. He gasped slightly, then deepened his kiss to an intensity that dizzied her.

Her mind spun into a dark world of sensation and yearning. She could no longer think. Reality consisted of darkness and Jarod and touch.

His fervent mouth on her own told her how much he wanted her. She was both thrilled and frightened.

His tongue traced and retraced the line of her upper lip with achingly sweet slowness. Her lips parted in a mixture of pleasure and longing so sharp it was like pain.

Then his tongue tasted her more boldly, more sensuously, more intimately. Shyly, hesitantly, she let the tip of her tongue touch his. The sensation was so enticing it seemed to shock her to another level of awareness.

You taste like warmth, she thought. *You taste like life. You taste like love.*

He made a sound of displeased restraint deep in his throat. With a motion so slow it seemed reluctant, he drew his hands from her back, moved them to her shoulders and began to push her coat softly off. His lips never left hers. She didn't want them to.

She forced herself to stop clinging to his neck long enough to extend her arms and let the coat slide soundlessly to the ground. She wound her arms around his waist. She felt his fingers on the top button of her shirt. It opened, and she sensed him touching the second button.

He spoke against her lips, his voice tense. "Stop me, Laura. For God's sake. Please."

She drew back just slightly, so that her trembly mouth barely touched his. *Yes. We have to stop. Now!* she wanted to say.

But she could say nothing, because he was kissing her again. Once again he was turning the world to darkness and touch, and all words were useless.

"I WONDER WHAT they're doing now," Susannah said wistfully. She and Gus sat at the kitchen table playing Scrabble. Aunt Mimi, tranquilized as usual, dozed in an armchair in the living room.

"Your beautiful sister is probably freezing her beautiful self to death in a tent. I should be there to warm her. Jarod? He's probably out on the ice doing push-ups. The guy's so Spartan. He's hopeless. He should learn to enjoy life."

Susannah's glasses slid down her nose. She pushed them back up with her forefinger. She studied Gus's complicated face, trying to fathom what emotions played behind his sleepy-eyed mask.

He looked calm, seemed confident. She, on the other hand, felt as if a thousand evil elves were nipping at her nerve ends with pincers.

"Why we haven't heard from them? Why hasn't there been any radio contact? Do you really think it's malfunctioned?"

"I'd lay money on it."

She fidgeted, smoothing her swept-back hair, which was perfectly smooth already. "But what if they *need* to get in touch? What if they find Tim, and he's hurt, and they need a helicopter to fly in for him? What if something happens to *them,* and they need help?"

"Nothing's going to happen to them. Jarod's in his element. If they need help he'll burn down a tree and send a smoke signal or something."

Gus set out his tiles to make a word on the Scrabble board. "Ah," he said with satisfaction. "Triple word score."

Susannah temporarily forgot her worries. She frowned at the board, wrinkling her nose. "*Quelp?* There is no such word as 'quelp,' Gus."

"Yes, there is," he said with assurance. "Ninety-six points."

She folded her arms on the table and stared at him militantly. "*Quelp?* You made that up. I'll prove it."

She reached for the dictionary. Gus sat back in his chair, completely poised and looking bored. "You won't find it. It's a new word, and that dictionary's twenty years old."

Susannah kept frowning as she looked in the *q*'s. "It's not here. It's not real."

"It's perfectly real," Gus said, adjusting a gold cuff link. "It's a grommet used in a fiber-optics board for quasar telemetry."

Susannah looked at him dubiously.

"You doubt me? Electronics is my profession—in part. Ninety-six points. Write it down."

She shook her head in disbelief, but added ninety-six points to his score. Then, as an afterthought, put a large question mark beside it.

"I'm deeply hurt that you doubt my honesty," he said.

Susannah underlined the question mark for emphasis. But she wasn't really thinking of the game.

"You really think the radio's only broken? Maybe they've had an accident of some kind."

He shrugged impatiently. "Equipment goes down all the time. They may already have Tim and be on their way back—right now."

She raised her eyes to his. His hooded gaze was steady. "Do you think so?"

He nodded. "It's possible. Hey, this is your brother we're talking about. You think I'd bring in a man for the job who was *de segunda categoria*—second rate?"

"No," she said softly.

"You think I'd let Laura go off with him if he wasn't first-class?"

"No," she said softly.

She looked at him lounging lazily in his chair. Did she only imagine that he was as uneasy as she, that in reality he was full of restless energy, coiled and waiting?

He was a deceptive-looking man. With his height and slimness and natural elegance, he *might* have had the blood of grandees in him. She could not blame Laura for having been fascinated by him.

She knew he could be dangerous and that his was a dangerous job. But paradoxically, her world felt safer because he was near, and she was glad of his presence.

He again was dressed as if he'd stepped out of a magazine ad. Somehow, he even managed to keep the cast on his wounded foot snowy white. When she'd expressed concern over his having been shot, he'd shrugged it off, saying it wasn't the first time. Susannah couldn't imagine anyone really being shot, least of all Gus. He seemed too neat to bleed.

"You must have been a strange pair, you and Jarod," she mused, leaning her chin on her hand.

"Strange? We were the Odd Couple. He said to dress for rough country. So I wore my jogging shoes—a hundred and forty dollars from L. L. Bean, too. He didn't tell me I needed hip boots. The swamp! The devil take it—the very frogs laughed at my misery. Huge savage frogs."

Susannah could not help smiling. "Tell me about it," she said.

And he did. He acted out the whole trip, making a comic opera of it. Although the journey must have been hellish, he mocked it at his own expense. Susannah, who had been almost sick with worry, laughed until her face ached.

"So what can I tell you?" Gus asked when he'd finished his epic recital. "Your sister and brother are in good hands. Granted, Jarod's crazy—he *likes* carrying a sixty-pound pack through a swamp—but he brought me back alive. He'll bring them, too. I promise you."

"You believe in him that much?" she said, slightly awed.

Gus's lean face went serious again. "He's a man of honor. I'd trust him with my life," he said.

"I CAN'T— YOU CAN'T— We can't—" Laura said against Jarod's lips.

"I know," he said. "I know."

He kissed her again.

She wanted to give herself to him completely, and she hated herself for wanting such a thing. It was so natural, she thought, so elemental. They were a man and a woman in the wilderness, and they desired each other.

Desire might be simple, she told herself desperately, but its consequences were complex. And here in the wilds, with no way to keep lovemaking safe...

She pushed away from Jarod, even though she loved being in his arms, adored the sensation of his mouth upon hers drinking away her reason, her will, her restraint.

"Laura..." he said raggedly.

"No," she said.

Her hand was on his chest, pressed against its warmth and muscled hardness. She forced her fingers to clamp into a fist, so she couldn't touch him with such yearning.

"Laura..."

"No," she repeated, tears springing to her eyes. "Oh, Jarod, you said to stop you. Stop. Please."

"Don't stop me," he said, trying to take possession of her lips again.

She ducked her face, eluding him. "Stop."

He kissed her tousled hair, the curve of her throat. "No. No."

She pushed at him feebly to thrust him away. "Yes."

He took her fist in his hand. He bent and kissed the inside of her wrist. Her pulse raced beneath his lips. "This has to happen," he said.

Her fingers wanted to open, to touch him with pleasure and acceptance. She clenched her fist more tightly. "Not here. Not now. *No*. You know it as much as I do."

Beyond the wilderness was civilization and a stern, complicated world, she told herself. They could ignore it only at their own peril. They were being crazy, they were being insane, irresponsible.

"*No*," she repeated, and marshaling all her willpower, she moved away from him.

He tried to take her into his arms again. She flinched away from him. He went motionless, his hands on her shoulders. He stared at her for a long tortured moment.

"My brother..." she said helplessly, not looking at Jarod. Tim was out there somewhere, cold, confused, suffering. She was seized by a superstitious fear. It seemed wrong, sinful, even, to take pleasure when Tim was at risk.

Jarod's hands tightened on her shoulders. "Your brother," he said, breathing hard. "And Gus."

Gus, she thought miserably. He always seemed to be with them, haunting them, thrusting himself between them like an intrusive ghost. But there was more to keep them apart than Gus.

"Just plain sense," she murmured unhappily. "I mean, reasonable people, responsible people don't..."

Words failed her. Once again his hands tightened on her shoulders. "No," he said, his voice husky. "They don't."

"We shouldn't. I don't even *know* you."

"You know me. You've known me from the start of time. And I've known you. Wanted you. Tried to find you. I'd given up. I thought I'd wanted something impossible."

"No."

"Yes," he said, trying to kiss her again. "I used to dream of you. Before I knew your name, your face. I used to think, 'I'll find you.' Wherever you were. Then I stopped believing. I believe again. I know you. I've always known you."

She let his lips brush hers, but then turned her face away, afraid of being overwhelmed. "You've kept me at arm's length. You've hardly spoken."

"I couldn't. I thought you were his. I promised him..." He didn't finish the sentence. His expression was almost anguished.

"You promised him what?"

"To... to speak on his behalf. He brought me here."

"Oh, Jarod," she said with an unhappy sigh. "Speak for yourself. I don't even know your first name."

"I'll talk to him," he said, gripping her more tightly. "I won't touch you again until I've talked to him." But he kept his hands clenched on her shoulders, as if he could not bear to let her go.

"Talk to *me*. Please," she begged. "Just talk. What's your name? Tell me."

He stared into her eyes. The firelight flickered on his face. "Michael. Michael Cross Jarod. My father named me for his friend. But his friend...took my mother. I don't use that name. My father couldn't stand to say it. Not after what happened. Not after she did what she did."

"Do you see me that way? As leaving one man for another?"

"I tried to. But no, I see you as you."

"Oh," Laura said, leaning her face against his chest. "Just hold me. Hold me and talk to me. Tell me everything. I want to know about you. Please...Michael."

"Don't. I can't use that name."

"I'm sorry. But talk to me. We won't do anything. Just let me know you. Have you ever let anyone know you?"

He took her in his arms. He stared into the fire. Hesitantly he began to talk. He told her about his mother's leaving, about his father and old Raymond Hare and Raymond, Jr. He told her about Wendy, all of it.

In turn, she told him about the events that had shaken her family: her mother's early death, the accident, losing her father and Tim's slow troubled road back to recovery.

She told him of the angry words she'd hurled at Tim, how she'd said she wanted a life of her own. She spoke of how guilty she felt, and Jarod held her and consoled her.

They talked half the night away. She felt as if all her life half her soul had been missing, and now, in Jarod, she had found it and was whole again.

HE AWOKE FIRST. She was in the sleeping bag because, at last, he'd made her take it. He stared at her face and almost smiled. He thought she was very beautiful in sleep.

He rose silently and fed the dying fire. Then he went to the mouth of the cave and stared outside. Dawn had just broken. Ice and frost still encased the trees and furred the ground. If the kid had moved since the ice storm, he would leave a visible path in the frost. They were closing in on him. Jarod could feel it.

But the dawn sky was cloaked with clouds, a white fog hugged the earth, and he sensed snow coming. If Tim was hurt or sick, there might be no way to bring a chopper in to pick him up. He had to get the kid back safe and well as soon as possible. He had to do it for Laura.

He closed his eyes and tried to visualize Tim. He willed himself to perfect stillness. He barely breathed. He concentrated.

But his mind's eye could see nothing except the same troubling thing it had seen since the search had started: a shifting gray mist without form or limit.

Help me find you, he thought fiercely, trying to focus on Tim. *Show me. Help me.*

But there was nothing, only the insubstantial mist. Then, suddenly, the other image appeared—Laura's eyes, full of tears. The vision vanished almost as soon as it appeared, but for the first time it frightened him.

Why did he keep seeing her that way? What brought those tears to her eyes? Grief? Pain? Hopelessness? What? He could not bear the thought of her tears.

He turned from the cave mouth and looked down at her again. He did not wonder that Gus had loved her. No, he did not wonder at all.

Gus. He didn't like thinking of Gus. He had betrayed him. The thought disturbed him deeply. He would have made love to Laura all night long if she hadn't stopped him.

He must not take her into his arms again. If he did, this time he might not be able to stop. That would be foolish and dangerous under the circumstances. It was also dishonorable. He needed to tell Gus first.

The damning thing was that he had broken his word. He could not forgive himself for that. He did not expect Gus to, either.

He filled one of the dented pans with water and put it on the fire to heat. He sat down beside Laura. He reached out to touch her hair, then stopped himself.

He looked away from her. Was this how Michael Cross had felt? Had he wanted Jarod's mother so much that it didn't matter what happened to others? Was this how Raymond, Jr. had felt? Had he desired Wendy so much that nothing had mattered—except her?

Troubled, he gazed at Laura again. He'd cursed other men for doing what he was doing now, feeling what he felt.

Her eyelids fluttered. She was awake. He inhaled sharply, his muscles tensing.

Her eyes opened, and she looked at him. His heart felt as if it was falling downhill and there was no way of stopping it.

She smiled. "Good morning," she said softly.

"Good morning."

"You look solemn."

"I've been thinking."

Her smile faded. Her expression looked frightened. "Of Tim?"

He nodded because it was at least partly true. "We'll find him today. I can feel it. But...I can't promise you how he'll be."

"You're worried about him, aren't you?"

He couldn't lie. "Yes."

"I am, too. I have this feeling that something bad is going to happen. I don't understand it. I just have the feeling."

He shrugged and shook his head, but he understood what she meant. He felt it himself. "We'll find him," was all he could say.

She studied him, worry in her eyes. He wanted to reach out, touch her face, but he didn't allow himself.

"You're worried about Gus, too, aren't you?" she said.

He looked away. "Yeah."

She was silent a moment. "I never really loved him. You know that, don't you?"

"I know. But he loves you. And he trusted me."

"That's what bothers you, isn't it? But we didn't plan for this to happen. It just did."

He said nothing. He heard the sleeping bag rustle. Out of the corner of his eye he saw her rise, leaning on one elbow.

"Do I still have to call you Jarod?" she asked softly.

He shook his head. "No."

"Jay? Would it bother you if I called you Jay—for your initial?"

"No." He didn't want to look at her, because she touched his feelings too deeply. "Maybe I understand better now," he said. "My mother, I mean. Raymond and Wendy, too. They were human, that was all. Maybe I can see why they did what they did."

"That's good...isn't it?"

"Yeah. That's good."

"Jay," she said, as if savoring the sound of it. "I like that. Like a wild bird, a bold, handsome bird. It's a good name—Jay."

He nodded. It gave him an odd pang when she said the name like that. He could only ease it by saying her name in return. "Laura," he said, but still he didn't look at her.

"Would you kiss me good-morning?" she asked, shyness in her voice.

He tensed again. He felt a muscle jump in his cheek. "I don't think that would be a good idea."

She was silent for a long moment. "Yes. You're right. I'm sorry."

"No," he said, meeting her eyes, "*I'm* sorry. But...I want this out in the open, laid on the table in front of Gus. You haven't wronged him. But I have. And I don't trust myself to touch you. I want you too much." He glanced unhappily about the cave. "But this isn't the time. Or the place."

She fell silent again. "I know," she said at last.

Restless, he turned toward the fire. The water was simmering. "We should get started," he said. "I think it's going to snow. That could mean trouble."

"Maybe he won't move on if it snows. That would help."

He nodded. "If he does move, with frost this thick, he'll leave a path. It'll be easier than reading a map."

"But if it snows?"

"That would be trouble."

She pushed aside the top of the sleeping bag and stood. She came to his side. He wanted to put his arm around her, draw her near, kiss her hair, then her temple, then her lips.

He wanted her so much he ached with it. But he must wait. First they had to find Tim. And then, once they were back, he had to talk to Gus.

GUS SAT IN THE KITCHEN, drinking a cup of tar-black coffee. Susannah leaned against the door frame, tightening the belt of her robe and trying to look nonchalant. "Do you always get up at dawn?" she asked.

He was dressed impeccably as usual. "I couldn't sleep," he said moodily, not glancing at her. "I keep thinking of her."

"Oh," she said, and looked away. She wondered what it would be like to have a man like Gus, mercurial and exotic, love her. She didn't suppose she would ever know. She was too dull, too ordinary, too bookish, not spirited like Laura.

"What do you think?" he asked, staring into his cup. "When it's over, will she have me? What do you think?"

I think she'd be a fool not to, Susannah thought with a rush of conviction that both surprised and shamed her.

"Who knows?" she said flippantly, shrugging. "Maybe she'll see the light."

"Maybe," he said somberly. "Maybe." He gave her a halfhearted smile. "You're a good kid, Suzie-Q."

She bit her lip. Nobody ever called her by a nickname, not ever. *I'm not a kid,* she wanted to say. *I'm a woman.*

She gazed out the window, instead. "It looks like snow," she said. "I wish they'd get back. I wish we'd hear from them. Tim . . . I keep thinking about him, out in the cold. I mean, I know you think this Jarod's infallible, but..." Her voice caught slightly.

Gus sighed and rose from the table. Hobbling, he came to her side. He put his arm around her, a brotherly gesture. Her glasses were, as usual, sliding down her nose. With his forefinger, he pushed them gently back into place.

"Hey," he said, putting his finger on the tip of her nose. "*No llores, piquita.* Don't cry, little sister. Perhaps today we'll both get our heart's desire."

Susannah stiffened in his casual embrace. Once again she tried to adopt a pose of flippancy. "The great Jarod will bring everybody home."

"Yes," he said and tapped her nose lightly. "He'll bring back the people we love."

She didn't want to look at him; she was afraid of what he might see in her eyes. She stared down at her foolish slippers that were shaped like bear paws. She felt strangely empty. "You really do, don't you? Love her, I mean?"

"*Es mi corazon,*" he said with feeling. "She is my heart." He kissed her on the forehead, then let her go.

CHAPTER NINE

It was as Jarod had promised. Tim had left a clear trail through the frost. Even Laura's untrained eye could pick it out.

By noon she was starting to dislike what she saw. She stopped, staring down at the frozen ground. The morning's mist had not burned off; it swirled around them like a cold curtain of gauze.

"His path—it's so irregular," she said apprehensively.

Tim's footprints were uneven and veered wildly first to the left, then to the right.

Jarod had hardly spoken since breakfast. "He's limping worse," he said, his face grim. "Staggering, too."

Laura's heart contracted with fear and pain.

"I'm sorry," he said.

"But he keeps going," she said, studying the erratic tracks in the frost. "Just like before. Is he pushing himself too hard?"

"Probably."

Tears, smarting, rose in her eyes.

Jarod put his arm around her. "He needs to get to food. He was doing what he had to do. He's got heart, your brother."

Oh, yes, Laura thought, trying to blink back the tears. *He's always had heart. But what if his strength fails? What if he's too confused to find shelter, food—what then?*

She squared her jaw. "Yesterday, you said there were signs that he stopped and rested—the way he should. I haven't seen anything like that today. Did he?"

Jarod seemed reluctant to answer. "No. It's like you said. He's pushing too hard."

"And that's a sign he's not thinking clearly, isn't it? He could exhaust himself."

He drew her closer, bent and kissed her hair. His nearness seemed to her the only emotional relief possible.

"Laura," he said, "don't think the worst. The kid's got a lot of determination."

"Yes, but he's determined to escape us."

"He can't for much longer. Come on, love. Let's find him."

She nodded. Did she imagine it, or had the fog thickened even as they stood there? It was impossible to see more than twenty feet, and the temperature was dropping.

Jarod drew his arm away, but he took her hand. Together they pressed on.

A half hour later, he made her stop. They sat in the shelter of a rocky ledge and shared jerky and dried fruit. Exhausted, Laura leaned against his chest for a moment. He held her gently, as if he read her fears. He said nothing. Perhaps he knew that words were useless until Tim was found.

Then he drew her to her feet, kissed her once, and they set out again. The fog had indeed thickened; it was turning into a blanket that obscured the world, and the world, closed in as it was, seemed eerily, unnaturally quiet. Tracking became increasingly slow, setting Laura's nerves even more on edge.

When Jarod suddenly stopped, she looked at him in alarm. He stared at the ground, his face more troubled than she had ever seen it. A forked vein played in his temple like a small bolt of lightning. He said nothing.

She followed his gaze to the frozen earth. The tracks, dim in the mist, seemed strange, but she did not understand why.

"What is it?"

He swore. "I knew it was happening," he said, his voice troubled. He swore again.

"Jarod, Jay, what is it?" she begged, putting one hand on his sleeve.

"That," he said, nodding at the welter of tracks. "Recognize anything?"

She shook her head in bewilderment, staring down at the confusing trail.

"He went in a circle, damn it," Jarod said with passion. "That means he was badly disoriented."

Laura's hand tightened convulsively on his arm. She stared at the tracks and saw what he meant. She'd heard stories about people lost in the woods who grew so confused they began to walk in circles, wasting their energy and getting no closer to safety.

Once she would have been unable to imagine such a thing happening to Tim; his woodlore was too good. But now he was making the most elemental of mistakes.

"Damn!" Jarod said savagely. "I was afraid of it. I could feel it happening. He must have crossed his own tracks at that talus. In that rock debris. I didn't want to believe it. I wanted to be wrong."

Laura raised her eyes to his in consternation. "Then he was getting lost. Badly lost."

He nodded, self-disgust engraved on his face. "I kept suspecting. I should have trusted instinct."

She squeezed his arm again. "The fog. We can hardly see six feet away. I can't tell *where* we are."

"Come on," he said, urgency straining his voice. "We're going to do double time. I don't like it, but we'd better."

He seized her hand again. She took a deep breath and followed, trusting him blindly.

Jarod's intensity transformed him into another kind of being. As the fog thickened, he moved at almost a crouch so as not to miss a single sign.

Laura felt as if they were lost in a gray-white nightmare. The very ground beneath her feet seemed insubstantial. Their path had become so erratic, swinging first this way, then that, she wondered if Tim had wandered in a fever.

Her own heart pounded painfully, her muscles ached, and her head hurt. But Jarod was relentless. He stayed on the trail, as capricious and illogical as it was, and drew her onward with him.

In that shifting gray-white mist, only three things seemed real: Jarod, physical exertion and her worries for Tim.

Her worst fear was that Tim, sick, weak, confused, had never made it to shelter, that he had collapsed somewhere in this hostile icy world.

He could have lain there all night, the warmth of life leaking away. He could be lying there still, frozen to death. The thought terrified her.

She did not know how long they pursued their zigzagging path. She tried to lose herself in prayers for Tim's safety. She had prayed little since her father's death and Tim's accident. Now in her mind, she carried on long, rambling, desperate petitions to heaven.

They half-climbed, half-slid down a slope so steep that Laura didn't see how Tim could have made it. She feared they would find him, crumpled lifeless, at its bottom.

They did not. Jarod paused for a moment, kneeling to examine the ground. When he stood again, she could see, even through the fog, how stony his face had become.

Once more he took her hand. They moved on, not climbing, but staying in the bed of the ravine.

Tim's course seemed straighter now, as if he'd been too weary to climb, but could only stumble along the valley.

The next time Jarod stopped, he again said nothing. He stared down where a litter of dark objects seemed to swirl in the shifting veils of fog. Once more he knelt. Her heart beating fearfully, she knelt beside him.

She recognized the things on the ground; they were Tim's. His blackened fry pan, his binoculars, flashlight, canteen. She reached hesitantly and picked up the canteen. It was heavy, half-full of frozen water.

His plastic tarp, haphazardly folded, also lay in the frost, along with the foam pad for his sleeping bag, a collapsible shovel and a garbage sack, loosely knotted.

Grimly Jarod unfastened the bag and opened it. It was partially filled with clothes, clean mixed with dirty. His eyes met hers.

"He had to lighten his load," she whispered brokenly. "It was too heavy for him, wasn't it?"

He retied the sack and nodded, his face worried. He said nothing.

Laura unfastened her waist strap and shrugged out of her pack. She opened it and began to stuff Tim's possessions into it.

"What are you doing?" Jarod asked, one dark brow drawing down.

"His things— I'll carry them. My pack's half-empty. He'll need these."

"Laura, you're carrying enough weight, and we're moving without rest. You should—"

"He's my *brother*," she said passionately, cramming the bag of clothes inside, then refastening the pack. "These are his things. He might need them." She struggled to swing the pack back into place.

In the stern line of his mouth, resignation mingled with concern. "Here," he said from between his teeth. "Let me help."

He hoisted the pack into place and adjusted the straps. He stood and offered her his hand. She took it and rose. Neither of them spoke again.

She knew what he was thinking: they must hurry.

THEY HAD PROGRESSED perhaps three-quarters of a mile from where Tim had unloaded the pack when they found the pack itself, cast carelessly against the base of a frost-rimed boulder.

As they stood looking at it, both mute, the first flakes of snow began to fall.

No, Jarod thought, his stomach knotting. *No. The trail will be covered.*

Wordlessly he checked the pack. The kid had taken his sleeping bag, his other canteen, his cooking pot. That was all. He'd left everything else behind.

Had he known where he was going? Did he believe he could get there if he didn't pack the extra weight? Did he know there was shelter and cached food nearby? Did he plan to return for the pack when he was rested and fed?

Or had he no longer known what he was doing? Had he been wandering aimlessly? And had he kept wandering until he'd dropped from exhaustion and hopelessness? Even now the snow could be covering his body.

He watched Laura stare at the pack. She seemed almost afraid to touch it, as if it were an evil omen.

Jarod hoisted it up and wedged it into the crotch of a pine tree where it would be at least partly sheltered. He drew a red bandanna from his hip pocket and tied it around one strap.

"We'll pick it up on our way back," he said with more confidence than he felt. "After we've got him."

She finally brought herself to speak. "Do you think he kept going until he collapsed?"

Jarod crouched and examined Tim's uneven tracks. He didn't want to tell Laura that she might be right. The kid might have given up and just lain down and slipped into a deadly sleep.

Jarod picked his words carefully. "If he keeps his head, he could be fine, even if he didn't make it to shelter. He's still got his sleeping bag. He can survive if he plays it smart." *If,* he thought ominously.

The snow began to fall more swiftly. It swirled around them, its whiteness mixing with the deepening gray of the fog. The fog was darker now because the unseen sun was sinking.

Jarod swore inwardly. He'd been sure he'd find the boy today—certain of it. But if the snow persisted and became heavier, he'd fail. And he didn't know what kind of shelter he could find for Laura and himself. He felt as if he were wearing a dirty white blindfold of cold, one that barely let him see the world.

He narrowed his eyes, and for a few feet followed Tim's trail at a crouch. He didn't like the way the kid had limped and staggered, didn't like it all. He didn't want to tell that to Laura.

He followed Tim's uneven tracks a few yards farther, then frowned, squinting up the blurred slope. The kid had clearly been exhausted at this point, but he'd taken the most difficult way and started going up.

Jarod stared through the gray fog and spinning snow. Why had Tim started climbing such a steep slope, tired as he was? Did he know something? Was there actually shelter up there, perhaps food, too? Or had he lost all rationality?

"He went up," he said quietly, not looking at Laura. "It's steep. Can you handle it?"

He heard her take a deep breath. "I'll handle whatever I have to," she said. Her voice shook. He was afraid to look at her. He didn't want to see the fear and sorrow he knew were written on her face.

He reached back toward her, waiting for her to take his hand. When she did, he held it tightly. "Come on," he said. "Let's go get him."

At that moment he knew, with sudden sickening certainty, that he was going to find Tim Finlay on that slope. That's what his intuition had been trying to tell him all along. The kid was up there somewhere in that shifting cloudy cold. And Jarod didn't have to look back to know that there were tears in Laura's eyes.

Yes, he thought, an eerie hollowness in his vitals, this was where they would find Tim. Maybe the kid really knew what he was doing and had spent his last strength to reach the safety of a cave. That, or the boy was dead.

Jarod climbed, holding Laura's hand, leading her as carefully as he could. He dreaded each step because each increased his uncertainty about what he would find.

Jarod knew an odd unpleasant fact. People wandering in the wilds almost always took a downward path, the one of least resistance, when they were struggling to survive.

But those who had chosen to die, those who had accepted doom as their lot, took the upward path.

Nobody knew why. But it was true.

"WHAT'S WRONG?" Laura asked, hanging on more tightly to Jarod's hand. The ravine's side was sheer, and once again she had the feeling she was climbing a cliff. The snow stung her eyes.

The frost made it hard to keep a foothold. Both she and Jarod kept sliding, slipping, scrambling. She was breathless with exertion, almost light-headed. She'd tried to pray, but it was as if her thoughts turned to vapor and drifted off into the encompassing fog.

Now, inexplicably, Jarod had stopped, although they had not reached level ground. She heard him utter an oath.

"What's wrong?" she repeated. "What is it?"

"I think it's a cave. Let me check it out. Are you all right? Don't try to move. I can't see five feet in front of me anymore. Just stay put, all right?"

"A cave?" she said, afraid to hope that Tim had actually reached safety.

"I think so. Stay here."

He released her hand. She clenched her fist in nervousness. He clambered upward to some sort of ledge. He hauled himself up, then disappeared from sight. The fog closed over everything, leaving her marooned and alone in a featureless world of killing cold.

She blinked against the blinding snow. She listened. In the unnatural quiet, she could hear only the ominous rush of the soft wind and the muted scrabble of gravel being displaced above her.

A few pebbles rained down, and she ducked them. She hunched against the chill, not knowing which was worse, the strain of climbing or, when she was still, the iciness that seeped into her bones.

Her pack seemed to weigh a thousand pounds, her feet were numb, and her wrists chafed. She heard more scrabbling above her. "Jarod?" she called, her voice shaking with cold and apprehension. "Jay? Answer me—please."

There was only the soft sibilance of the wind. Once more she had to blink the snow from her eyes. Jarod didn't answer.

She leaned more wearily against the steep, bent her head and lay her forehead against her snowy sleeve. This was what hell was like, she was certain. Hell wasn't heat and flames and hordes of laughing imps. Hell was this loneliness, this fear and this ceaseless soul-killing cold.

"Laura!" Jarod's strained voice, almost directly above her, startled her. "Give me your hands. Be careful. This ledge is weak. It crumbles."

She reached up to him eagerly. "Is he here? Is it really a cave?"

"Concentrate. Be careful."

This time she didn't fight him when he drew her upward. She gritted her teeth and hung on as hard as she could. The rocky ledge, its edge deteriorating as he pulled her over, rained down shards of stone that rattled down the steep.

But then, miraculously, she was on the ledge. Jarod pulled her away from its treacherous rim. He stood, drawing her to her feet. They were at the mouth of another crevice, almost five feet tall. It was narrow, but not so narrow that a man without a pack might enter.

Jarod had shed his pack. Wordlessly he stripped hers off and set it on the ledge beside his. He took his flashlight, switched it on and stepped through the narrow opening. He reached for her hand and drew her after him.

She could not bear to ask the questions that obsessed her. She swallowed hard, feeling as helpless as a person slipping from one bad dream into another.

By the flashlight's dim glow, the cave seemed a dank and gloomy place, colder than the other two.

She heard the gurgle of water, and it gave her hope. She looked up. There was a hole perhaps two feet in diameter in the cave's roof, and snow fell through it. They must be just under the crest of the ravine, because through the hole she saw a patch of gray sky. A sulfurous-smelling lukewarm mist permeated the air.

She shut her eyes tightly, afraid to look any more closely. Her knees were weak, shaking.

Jarod's arms closed around her, firm and supportive. She wanted to bury her face against his chest.

"No," he whispered. "It's all right. He's here. He's alive. Prepare yourself, because he doesn't look good. But he's alive. That's what counts."

Again, she did not feel real. His words seemed like words from a dream, quickly fading, their message lost.

He squeezed her again. "Look," he ordered.

She opened her eyes. Jarod's light played on the far corner of the cave. A strange spring bubbled up from the highest part of the uneven floor, trickled for a short distance, then disappeared again into a crease in the stone. When snowflakes struck the flowing water, it steamed slightly.

Through its mist, she saw a bundle, partly hidden by drifted leaves. The bundle was Tim's sleeping bag. He lay in it, motionless.

Her mouth went dry; her knees sagged, but Jarod held her fast, and with his touch he seemed to be willing her strength back into her. "No, Laura, he's alive."

The figure moved slightly. It murmured unhappily, a sound so weak it might have been made by a child. Then it emitted a cough, dry and rasping.

"Tim?" she said, as if he were a phantom who might turn into mist and vanish. "Tim?"

Her only answer was another cough.

Afterward she was never able to remember clearly what happened next. The only thing she could recall was being on her knees beside Tim, embracing him with all her might.

She held him in her arms and cried, great racking sobs. He seemed to awake, to try to hold on to her in return. She kissed him and was alarmed that his skin was so cool and clammy.

She hovered over him, studying his face. He'd lost a frightening amount of weight in the time he'd been gone. His lips were cracked, his face smudged with dirt and soot, and he needed a shave.

He blinked up at her, at first not seeming to recognize her. "Laura?" he said at last in a ragged shaky voice. "I d-don' feel good. Tell Dad . . . I can't go . . . church, huh? Huh?"

Then he closed his eyes, something almost like a smile on his lips, and his head sank back to rest against her breast once more.

"Oh, my God," she said, her tears flowing, "he's delirious." She held him more tightly and rocked him as if he were a child. She pressed her cheek against his hair. His speech had been more slurred than usual—a bad sign.

Then Jarod was beside her, the first-aid kit open. He stirred Tim back to wakefulness. He made him swallow water and somehow got aspirin down his throat. He bathed his face with warm water from the spring.

Laura took the boy's temperature. It was 94.5—on the dangerous edge of hypothermia.

Jarod unzipped the sleeping bag to examine Tim further. Laura gasped with sympathy for her brother. He still wore his jacket, which was filthy, and both elbows were ripped and with blood.

The knees of his jeans were torn away, the skin beneath them badly cut and scraped.

"No," he said feebly when Laura and Jarod worked to strip away his ruined clothing and clean his wounds. But he was too weak to fight them. Laura quickly tended his wounds, and they managed to dress him in the clothes she had rescued from along the trail.

She bundled him into Jarod's parka and took his ruined one for herself. She zipped him back into his own sleeping bag, then went to get Jarod's from his pack.

Jarod, building a fire, warned her to be careful of the ledge. "This cave's so weathered it's fragile," he said, looking up at the hole in its roof. "I'll bet its ceiling was still intact last time he was here. This rubble—" he nodded at the littered floor "—is fairly fresh."

Picking her way carefully, she got the sleeping bag, unzipped it and covered Tim with it. He had the recurring shudders of a hypothermia victim, and she wanted to ease them.

Jarod joined her as soon as the fire flared brightly. She stroked Tim's brow and gazed at him in concern.

"What do you think?" Jarod asked. He, too, stared down at Tim's pallid face.

"He doesn't have pneumonia—yet," she said, still running her hand across the boy's forehead. "But he may be getting bronchitis—I don't like the sound of that cough. And he's suffering from exhaustion. And hypothermia. I'm surprised it's not worse."

"I'm making him soup and tea. As soon as he's eaten, get him up and moving. We've got to get his circulation going."

"Right," she said. "Get warm stuff inside him. Make him move. When he rests, make sure he's close to the fire. But what I don't understand are his knees—his knees and hands and elbows. Why are they so cut up?"

Jarod rose and went back to the fire. "He's a brave kid, Laura. He crawled the last two hundred yards or so. It must have been hell. I didn't want to tell you."

She winced and found herself blinking back tears again. "But he made it. He didn't give up."

"No. And neither can we." He went to his pack and brought back his groundsheet cover. He spread it near the fire. Then he went to Tim, scooped him up, sleeping bags and all, and carried him to the spot near the fire.

Laura roused the boy and made him sit. When he tried to slump back to the ground, she held him up stubbornly.

Jarod brought her a cup of soup and another of tea. Tim refused to hold a cup himself, so Laura fed him as if he were a child. At first he resisted, then he seemed to accept her ministrations, even welcome them.

Jarod brought her two more mugs and a chunk of jerky. "Let me feed him. You should eat, too."

She shook her head. "He knows me. I've got him. Go ahead. You eat."

He looked at her holding the cup to her brother's lips. Then he nodded. He sat down cross-legged beside her. He ate in silence and with a strange air of determination.

"If only we hadn't broken the radio," Laura fretted, urging Tim to take another drink of soup.

She didn't know how much of the conversation Tim could understand, and she didn't want him to be frightened. She tried to send Jarod the message with her eyes: *I'm worried. This is an emergency. He needs help as soon as possible.*

Jarod seemed to understand. He nodded, then stared up at the hole in the cave roof. "The radio would have made no difference. Not right now. No aircraft could take off in this. Nobody could get to us."

He set his jaw. "Look," he said, turning back to Laura. "We're going to have to make this place as tight and warm as possible. I'm going to try to block that hole in the roof— with his groundsheet. You still have yours, right?"

"Yes." She sensed he was planning something, but she didn't understand what.

He nodded toward the cave's narrow opening. "I'll try to rig a curtain to keep some of the cold out, too. There's a little wood here. I'll gather more."

His uneasy gaze fell on Tim again. "Has he finished that tea? Give him more. Then let's walk him. We've got to get his temperature up."

Laura nodded, bit her lip in concentration as she poured and sugared more tea. She made Tim drink again, then she and Jarod helped her brother rise unsteadily to his feet. He tried to sag back to the ground, but Jarod forced him to stay upright.

"Walk, kid," Jarod ordered with such force that Tim struggled to straighten himself. For a moment the boy's eyes seemed to clear. He stared at Jarod with dazed interest.

"You..." he said groggily to Jarod. "Y-you—the angel of death?"

"No, kid," Jarod said from between his teeth. "I just came along with the angel of life over there." He nodded toward Laura, who held Tim up from the other side. "Now, walk, damn it."

Tim walked. Feebly. But he walked.

CHAPTER TEN

AFTER THEY WALKED Tim around the cave, they sat him down by the fire again, and Laura made him drink more hot liquid.

Again she said how sorry she was the radio had been ruined. She blamed herself.

Jarod said it was no one's fault, and she musn't feel that way. They would have to do what they could by themselves.

He made a curtain out of a groundsheet at the cave mouth to block the draft. Then he went into the darkness and cold, and somehow, with heavy branches and the other groundsheet, he blocked the hole in the cave roof.

When he returned, he was covered with snow, his face red with cold, but he bore an armload of firewood. He set it by the flames to dry. He wore no jacket, only a windbreaker over his vest.

Against Laura's protests, he went back into the bitter night for more wood. He went repeatedly. He didn't stop until he had stacked what seemed to her an inordinate amount.

"Sit down," she pleaded at last, catching his gloved hand. The coldness of the snow on it stung her fingers. "You're going to be in worse shape than Tim if you don't rest."

She nodded at her brother. She held him in her arms, his back against her chest, his head on her shoulder. She'd wrapped him in both sleeping bags. He shivered less than before, and when she'd last taken his temperature, it had risen almost a degree and a half.

He was far from well; when conscious, he seemed still in some sort of a daze. She intended to wake him at least once an hour, forcing him to drink warm liquids and walk.

His chill, she knew, was far deeper and more dangerous than hers had been after her fall into the creek. Her skin and extremities had felt frozen, but Jarod had treated her immediately.

Tim, in contrast, had lain alone and untended, growing cold to his very core. His internal organs needed warming, and merely cuddling with him might draw blood away from them. He needed to be rewarmed at his center with hot food and drink and exercise, as much as he could take.

She meant to see that he did what needed to be done. But now she worried about Jarod; he seemed to be pushing himself needlessly to increase the wood supply.

She squeezed his hand. "Please," she said. "You're covered with snow. Rest. Have another cup of tea."

He sighed, either in weariness or resignation, then nodded. He took off his hat, stripped off his gloves and jacket, setting them by the fire to dry. He poured himself a cup of tea.

He sat beside her. She held Tim and smiled at Jarod. He seemed to try to smile back, but the smile never reachèd his eyes and quickly died from his lips.

"Rest," she repeated, looking fondly at him. "You've earned it. You found him. It's like a miracle. Now we just have to signal for help."

He stared into the fire. When he spoke, it was without emotion. "I looked at the supplies he cached here. He never touched them. Too exhausted probably. He's got six cans of soup, two of tuna, one of peanuts, a couple cans of apple juice."

She nodded, wondering why he seemed so solemn. The news was good; they had plenty of food.

The firelight danced on his features. The frown line between his brows deepened. "Between my stuff and his, you should be fine for at least another four, maybe five days. You can melt snow if you need more water. But be sure to boil it."

His unexpected statement filled her with anxiety. She hugged Tim to her more tightly. "What do you mean?"

"Listen to me," he said almost harshly. "This snow isn't going to stop. There's no way we can signal anybody. And nobody can get to us."

"What—do you mean?" she repeated. An inner coldness, more hellish than any imposed from the outside, possessed her.

"I'm going for help," Jarod said. "Alone."

He turned and met her gaze, his eyes holding hers. He was always intense, and she had never seen him more so than at this moment.

"No..." she started to protest.

"Don't argue," he said harshly. "Listen."

Frightened by his tone, she waited for him to go on.

He drew a deep breath. "This snow isn't going to stop—"

"You don't know that. You *can't* know. It might stop by morning. We can send a signal—"

"No," he said as fiercely as before. "I *do* know. It has that feel. If it was only you and I, we could wait it out. But with him like this—" he nodded grimly at her brother "—we can't wait."

"But—"

"Somebody has to go for help. It can only be me. You stay here. Take care of him. You know what to do. Keep him warm, fed. Make him walk."

She looked at him numbly. "You can't go back, not now. It's dark."

"I can start. I can travel fast if I travel light."

She looked at him, appalled. "It's suicide. We could barely see in the daylight. By night it's impossible."

"It's not. I know where we are—almost dead center of the wilderness area. Your place is due south. If I follow the ravine, I'll be headed for it. Even if I miss your place, I'll come out close to civilization. It's just a question of walking."

"No," she begged. "Not in the dark. You could get turned around like Tim did. You could fall into a ravine and break something. Or into a creek like I did. The fast-flowing ones won't be frozen yet. You could—"

He put his finger on her lips to silence her. "I'll be careful. I won't get turned around. I'll have Tim's compass—you saved it, remember?"

"But—"

"Shh," he said, now laying two fingers on her lips. "I've got two flashlights—because of you. His and mine. And extra batteries. I can make it, Laura. I know I can."

"You'll freeze!"

"No. I'm used to cold. And I'll keep moving." His fingertips caressed her mouth.

"But if something happens to you—"

"Nothing will happen."

"But if it does—"

"As soon as it clears, build a fire outside and signal. Keep signaling until they find you. And take care of Tim. That's your job."

"I don't want you to go," she said. Tears welled in her eyes. One spilled onto her cheek. He brushed it away.

"I have to. It's the only way," he said, his forehead creasing as he nodded at Tim. "Right now the only way to get him out of here is by carrying him."

"We could carry him together," she said desperately. "Rest and wait until morning. We'll all go. I can help."

"You can't. You're too small, and the country's too rough."

"Let me *try*."

Another tear spilled, creeping down her cheek. Frowning harder, he wiped it away. "Do you really think he could survive the exposure? With just you and me trying to get him back?"

She shrugged helplessly. She knew he was right. Carrying Tim, Jarod couldn't choose the shortest path. He would have to choose the one over which a sick man could be borne. Laura could help support Tim if he could keep walking on his own. But he couldn't. And with the ice and snow? Jarod would have to carry him in his arms like a child. Their progress would be slow, and every moment would take its toll on Tim.

"Listen," Jarod said, "this snow, this fog—it feels like it could last another full day, maybe two."

She kept her grip on his shoulder. "Another day or two? Then stay here. We can wait it out."

He glanced at her hand for a long moment, as if memorizing it. "Laura," he said, meeting her eyes again, "it *could* last longer. The safest thing is for me to go. Now. As soon as I can get help, I'll start back for you, but with a party, with the equipment to get Tim out of here fast."

"But you'll be exhausted. What if you can't find us?"

"I will find you. I'd never lose you. Never. But I have to go. As soon as possible."

"I don't like it," she said, trying to keep her jaw from trembling. "I don't want you to—"

He ignored her words. "In the meantime," he said, "if the weather clears, I'll send the helicopter for you."

Her mind spun, dizzy with a whole host of new fears. Tim *did* need medical help. He couldn't stand more exposure. If

Jarod was right and the snow and fog persisted, there was no way for anyone to get to them by air. And by foot, no searcher could find them—unless Jarod told them the way. Yet the chance he was taking terrified her.

"If I set out now, moving fast, I might make it by morning—with luck. I could be back for you by nightfall. We could get Tim out of here and into a hospital where he belongs."

"But when will you rest?"

"When you're safe."

"But you've been moving and working since dawn. You can't travel all night, then come back for us—you'll kill yourself."

"I can do it for you."

"But how can I stand it," she asked, her fingers digging possessively into his shoulder, "knowing you're out there alone and in danger? I can't."

"You can because you have to. For your brother's sake. It's going to take both of us to save him."

She stared at him, her eyes burning with unshed tears. "I'm afraid."

"Don't be," he said. "I'll be thinking of you every minute. That'll be my magic. That'll make me invulnerable."

She wanted to sink against his chest, to cling to him as tightly as she was able, but she could not. She held Tim and had to keep on holding him.

Jarod, his hand gently framing her jaw, tilted her face toward his. He bent and kissed her so sweetly it shook her to her heart, then he drew away. He lifted his hand to his throat and took off the beaded necklace with the medicine bag.

"Look," he said gruffly, "I know you don't believe in this. But I'd feel better if you wore it for me—all right?"

He started to slip the necklace on her, but she caught his hand and shook her head, almost unable to speak. "No.

You wear it. Please. Don't take it off. I'll be worried sick about you if you do."

He hesitated, his hand caught in hers. She looked into his eyes. "Please," she repeated. "Don't take it off. It might mean bad luck. Keep it with you—for me. Promise."

Something half-sad yet still close to a smile flickered at the corners of his mouth. Her hand tightened on his, and he bent and kissed her fingers. Then he nodded. "If you want it that way," he said.

"I want it that way."

He slipped the necklace back on over his head and tucked it beneath his shirt. He took her hand and kissed it again. Then he bent once more and pressed his lips to hers.

At that moment Laura wished that both of them could leave their separate identities, their separate bodies, and merge into one entity, dazzling in its completeness, perfect in its rightness.

For a few seconds, it seemed almost as if her wish had been granted. She felt as if she was a part of Jarod and he a part of her, and that the miracle sent a tremble through the universe.

Then he drew away, leaving her merely human again, bereft and alone. Once more he placed his finger against her lips. "I won't tell you goodbye," he whispered. "I'll never tell you that. So take care, Laura. Of yourself and your brother. We'll be together again as soon as I can make it happen."

Reluctance marked his face as he drew farther away from her, then stood. He reached to the hawk feather on his button and untied it. "Here," he said, holding it out to her. "At least keep this for me—so I fly like a hawk back to you."

She took it, unconsciously holding it next to her heart as she stared up at him. "Jarod," she said, her throat tight, "take the jacket I've got on—Tim's. I know you won't take your own—" she glanced at Tim, who was still bundled into Jarod's jacket "—but take this one. It's got rips in the sleeves, but it's heavier than the vest you're wearing. Please."

"I'm better off in this," he said, zipping up the windbreaker. "The rips in that would let warm air out. I'll be fine if I keep moving."

He slung the smallest canteen over one shoulder. He filled one pocket with a package of jerky and a bag of trail mix. In the other, he put Tim's small flashlight and all the extra batteries.

Pretend he's not leaving, Laura told herself. *Pretend he's just going away for a little while, gathering more wood, that's all.*

She resisted the impulse to turn away and shut her eyes so that she wouldn't have to see him go. She wanted to drink in every detail of him: his height, his leanness, his keen gray eyes shadowed by the hat's wide brim, the stern beautiful line of his jaw.

He looked at the ground, not at her. She wondered if it hurt him as much to leave as it hurt her to see him go.

He moved to the cave opening. When he drew aside the makeshift curtain, a chilly gust of wind entered, making Laura shudder and Tim stir uneasily in her arms.

Still Jarod didn't turn to meet her eyes. "Take care," he said in a tightly controlled voice. "I'll see you soon."

He pushed the curtain farther aside. Laura felt the frigid edge of the wind, heard its keen. For a moment she could not speak. Then she managed to repeat his words, "Take care," she whispered brokenly. "I'll see you soon."

Then the curtain fell back into place, and he was gone. They had both tried to act as casually as if he was taking a stroll to the corner store.

But she knew the sort of danger he was stepping into. They hadn't said goodbye. They said, almost superstitiously, only, "I'll see you soon."

She sat holding Tim and listening to the wind howling outside. She was sure, somehow, that she and Tim would hang on, that they would be saved, and that she owed her brother's life to Jarod.

But she was frightened for Jarod's own chances and in truth did not know if she would ever see him again.

She sat, staring after him, sitting in a small cave by a small fire, a sick boy in her arms and, for hope, one single feather in her hand.

"God go with you, Jarod," she whispered.

THE NIGHT WAS the longest Laura had ever known. She woke Tim, who grew increasingly irritable each time she did. When he was conscious, he was not completely rational. Once he slapped the mug from her hands, pitching tea into the fire so that the flames sputtered and sank.

She'd wanted to shake him, but reminded herself that he was sick and disoriented. She had lost patience with him once before, and now they were all paying a terrible price for it—especially Jarod, out there in the cold and darkness.

So she kept forcing Tim to eat and drink. By a combination of cajoling, wheedling and threatening, she made him get to his feet and pace the cave. "You've got to," she kept saying.

Sometimes he seemed close to rebellion, but some deeper part of his mind must have understood and he obeyed.

By morning, she was exhausted, but his temperature was almost normal again. Outside the wind's howl was weaker, and at times it nearly died.

She made Tim powdered eggs laced with chunks of dried ham. For the first time he ate hungrily, and he drank tea and hot apple juice by himself.

Although he clearly did not feel well yet, he'd begun to sound like himself. They had their first lucid conversation.

He held his mug and stared into the fire. His words came haltingly, as they had since the accident. "I w-was afraid. That you w-w-w-mad. Were mad. At me. W-wouldn't want me. Wouldn't want me back."

She put her hand on his thin shoulder. "We wanted you back. Very much. We love you."

He shook his head unhappily. "I wa-wanted come... home. But I didn't—didn't think you want me. I think you are... mad. Because I run 'way. Because I run away."

She wound her arm around his neck. She leaned so that her head rested against his. "It was my fault you felt bad enough to run away. I was mad at myself, not you. We love you. We want you home."

He was silent a moment. His cup was empty, and he set it down. When he spoke, hesitancy tinged his voice. "Laura?"

"Yes?"

"You m-made me mad."

"I know. I'm very sorry. We... we have to learn to be patient with each other."

"Laura?"

"Yes?"

"I run 'way... run away because of what you say... said to me."

Her arm tightened around his shoulder. "I know. I'm sorry, Tim."

He raised his hand to his forehead, touched it gingerly. "And now?" he said, sounding chagrined. "You know? I c-can't remember what you say. W-what you said. I can't even remember why I ran... away."

"Oh, Tim," she said, saddened by the irony, "it's best forgotten. Let it stay forgotten."

She took his face between her hands and kissed him at the edge of his mouth. He wound his free arm around her shoulders and hugged her. For a moment they clung together, sister and brother, neither able to speak, and Laura blinked back tears.

"When I c-came into the...woods," Tim said, his cheek pressed against hers, "I did...didn't care if I live or die out here. But then...it got bad. And I knew then. I want...to live. I wanted to live. So bad. So much. I— That's what the w-woods taught me."

She hugged him tighter. "Then they taught you the right thing. You're going to live. And get well. You were so brave and so smart. You survived. We're together again. And we'll be going home—soon."

He drew back, clearly embarrassed by the show of emotion. "Snowing?" he said gruffly, staring into the fire again.

"Yes. It's snowing."

"I...got us in...one damn fix, huh?"

She smiled one-sidedly and put her hand on his shoulder again. "It's a pretty good fix. But we'll get out. You'll see."

He pushed his hand through his dark tangled hair. "The man," he said, frowning to himself. "Who? Where?"

She took a deep breath. Pain cracked across her heart, wrenching it. "His name is Jarod," she said, her voice tight. "He's a tracker. He found you. But you led him a merry chase."

He frowned harder. "Ja-rod? I n-never heard of him. How...how'd he come to here? To be here. With you? For me?"

How'd he come to be here? With you? For me? she mentally echoed. The answer should have been simple and elegant: *He came here to me, for you, by a miracle.*

But in truth the answer was neither simple nor elegant, and it was one she preferred to forget. But to forget would be dishonest.

"Gus Raphael," she said reluctantly. "You remember Gus? Gus knew Jarod. He brought him—clear from Maine."

Tim laughed wryly. "Gus Raphael? Gus? You . . . gonna take him back f-finally?"

She shifted uncomfortably. "Of course not."

"Gus int . . . isn't a b-bad guy."

She sighed. For an instant, her brother seemed like his old teasing self. She only wished he hadn't become so on the touchy subject of Gus.

"He's not such a bad guy," she admitted grudgingly. And she supposed he wasn't. He had brought them Jarod, and Jarod had given Tim back into their keeping.

And now Jarod was risking his life for them. All the fears she'd harbored yesterday for her brother were transferred to Jarod. Was he safe? Or was he suffering, hurt, fallen and freezing in some forsaken place?

She could not bear such thoughts. For the thousandth time she regretted the loss of the radio. But regret helped nothing.

She rose and tugged Tim by his jacket. "Stop talking," she ordered. "Start walking. We're going to pace this cave 150 times."

Tim moaned in protest. "Laura, no! I . . . don't feel so g-good. Can I . . . can't I just sleep?"

"No," she said, all business and toughness. "I want that temperature right back up. Walk—hut, two, three, four."

They paced the gloomy cave until Laura herself was sick of it, and only then did she let him get back into the sleeping bag. He wriggled away from her in disdain when she tried to make him lay his head in her lap.

He must be feeling better, she thought ruefully; he was starting to act like a little brother again. She huddled close to the fire, wrapping herself more tightly in his torn coat. She hoped she could sleep.

Her night had been long, her sleep sporadic, and when she let herself think, her thoughts flew to Jarod and made her so fearful she felt sick to her stomach.

She dozed, but had nightmares that Jarod was hurt and helpless. She awoke and checked Tim. He seemed groggy, listless. She took his temperature, and when she read it, her concern for him flared anew.

Somehow, in his sleep, his temperature had crossed the line from low to high. He was feverish now. She fed him more soup, more apple juice, but didn't make him walk. He was starting to have coughing spells. She thought it best he rested.

She made him take aspirin, then let him settle into the sleeping bag again. He fell back to sleep almost immediately, but his forehead was starting to glisten with sweat.

Oh, heavens, she thought in panic and weariness, *now he's going to get pneumonia. Oh, hurry, Jarod. Come back and get us. Be well and come back to us. Please, oh, please.*

She could not fall asleep again. She checked Tim, she checked the weather. The snow had stopped, the fog had thinned, but not lifted. Frost still filmed the ledge, and through the shifting mists, she could hear the twigs and tree limbs popping from the weight of the ice.

What time was it? she wondered. It seemed past noon, but she couldn't be sure. Where was Jarod? Had he made it home safely? Was he at this moment on his way back to them as he had promised?

She could only pray that he was. Tim's fever was climbing, she could tell. He had started to have the shakes again, now from the chills that marked the valleys between the peaks of his fever.

She woke him, gave him an aspirin and another dose of the precious antibiotics. He stayed awake for some time, but his mood was dark again, and she knew he was frightened.

His coughing grew worse, and she was relieved when he fell into a relatively peaceful sleep.

The afternoon lengthened. It seemed to lengthen into an eternity. *At any minute the sky will clear,* she told herself. *The sky will clear, and the helicopter will arrive, and the rescue workers will come down to us like delivering angels and bear us back to safety—and to Jarod.*

But the sky did not clear.

MERCIFULLY LAURA DOZED again, but when she awakened, it was with the skittish instinct that something was very wrong.

A sound had woken her. A sound that didn't seem human—a scratching and growling behind the curtain at the cave mouth.

She rose on her elbow, the back of her neck prickling. She heard the scratching again. Something growled, then gave a low ill-tempered whine.

Her senses surged to a higher level of awareness. The noises were sinister yet mockingly familiar, as well.

Oh heavens, she thought, her alarm rising, *a wild dog. Maybe more than one.*

Wild dogs scavenged and hunted the edge of the wilderness area. They found farm animals easier prey than those of the forest. But even the wild dogs had their renegades, and a few, she knew, ranged into the heart of the forest.

Now that the snow had stopped, a wild dog—likely drawn by warmth and the scent of food—was on their doorstep. Perhaps, she thought sickly, more than one dog.

Again there was scratching at the curtain and a deep-throated sound between a whine and growl.

Laura scrambled to her feet, looking frantically around for a weapon. The wild dogs were shy—they did not like people. But they were cunning, too, and could sense cowardice or weakness. It was rare for them to attack humans—but it had happened.

Tim had a hunting knife that lay by the fire. She snatched it up, drawing it from its sheath. She felt both terrified and ridiculous—she had never wielded a weapon in her life. If the dog leapt at her, could she actually use the knife?

Fire, she thought, trying to think as cagily as a wild animal herself. Wolves were frightened of fire—wouldn't dogs be, as well?

With her other hand she grabbed a brand from the fire. It was a limb not quite two feet long, strong and solid, its end burning brightly.

Stealthily she moved to the mouth of the cave. There was a moment of silence, then a growl that seemed half wary, half warning.

I can't be cowardly, she told herself, gritting her teeth. *My brother's sick and helpless.*

With her knife hand, she thrust back the curtain and lunged forward, holding the burning torch before her.

The dog sprang backward, its hind legs skidding on the ledge. Its body tensed and its muzzle wrinkled as it snarled, baring its teeth. It was an ugly blackish-brown dog of medium size, its coat partly winter-thick and partly ragged with mange. There was something close to madness in its eyes, and it crouched as if to attack.

Laura's reflexes took over. She struck at the dog. It dodged the blow, but crouched again, showing its teeth and growling. She wondered, in panic, if it was crazed with cold or hunger or disease.

It darted toward her, snapping at her ankles. Gathering her strength, she swung again. This time the blow connected.

There was a solid thump of contact, the dog's maddened yelp, and the brief stench of burning fur on the cold air. The dog shrieked and turned tail. Laura swung at it again, determined to drive it away once and for all.

The dog, yipping and howling, fled across the frosty slope. Scuttling to keep its balance on the steep ground, it disappeared into the fog.

"And stay away!" Laura cried after it furiously. She didn't think she'd hurt the dog, only frightened it. She threw the brand after it as hard as she could, although she knew she'd never hit it.

But even as she flung the burning stick, she realized her mistake. Her balance shifted to her left foot, the foot nearest the ledge.

Simultaneously the ground beneath her foot disintegrated.

Part of the rock fragmented into shards and pebbles that rattled down the steep like hail. Laura found herself doing a helpless dance, first on stone, then on air.

She heard the fleeing yips of the dog as she lost her balance and pitched off the crumbling ledge.

Then the frozen ground seemed to slam into her, knocking her breath away with such force she could not even gasp in pain. She was sliding headlong down the ravine's sheer side, unable to stop her plunge.

At last, rolling and flailing, she hit the trunk of a tree. She struck it sideways, and with a stab of pain she knew immediately she'd broken a rib, perhaps two.

She lay stunned, the pain shooting through her chest so fierce she wondered if she had punctured a lung. She could not get her breath. She tried to scream, but the sound was a weak helpless cry from the back of her throat.

Tim, she thought frantically, *I've got to get back to Tim.* Her ungloved fingers scrabbled at the frozen earth as she tried to pull herself back up toward the cave. But the pain pierced through her side again so sharply she moaned.

She seemed to rise above her own body and float there, staring down at it dispassionately. She was a small woman in a torn oversize coat, knotting herself into a ball of pain. Her hair lay in a red-gold tangle against the snow, and her eyes were squeezed tightly shut.

Up the slope—she did not even know how far—her brother lay in a feverish sleep. He did not know she was gone. He would probably kill himself if he came looking for her and tried to drag her back to the shelter of the cave.

The fog swirled around her like thin scarves. The sun was going down. The snow burned coldly against her cheek, but she had no strength to turn from it.

Jarod had said he would be back by nightfall. But night was falling, and there was no sign of him. With perfect clarity she knew that if Jarod hadn't found help that morning, none of them might make it. If he didn't come soon, she'd be dead from exposure.

"Jarod," she whispered, but uttering the word caused her such pain that her mind turned to blackness.

Somewhere in the distance, a wild dog howled.

And softly, once again, the snow began to fall.

CHAPTER ELEVEN

A GIGANTIC CLATTERING filled the air. Laura wanted to turn from it. The noise was painful, and she was tired of pain. She wanted only to sleep. Far away, barely audible under the clatter, was a soft warm rumble, like spring thunder.

No, not thunder, the voices of men.

Hands pulled at her, hurting her, trying to drag her from the safe fortress of her sleep. The hands plucked at her clothes, and she wanted to slap them away, but she hadn't the strength.

Then the hands were binding her ribs. They bound her chest once, twice, three times, so that the bandages overlapped slightly. *My ribs are broken,* she thought dully. *And they're bandaging me to move me. I don't want to move. I just want to sleep.*

"Don't let her go back to sleep," a strange voice said. Someone slapped at her cheeks smartly. Irritation warred with numbness for her consciousness.

Someone slapped at her again, and irritation won. The clattering sound above her grew until it was loud enough to wake the dead. *Or the dying,* her confused mind thought, vaguely startled.

The men's voices were talking to her, but she could not understand them for the insane clatter. The hands, so maddeningly pesky, transferred her to some sort of stretcher, strapping her to it.

She had a strange sensation; she was being drawn upward, swaying slightly, into the very heart of the clatter. She thought that perhaps this was what dying was. Angels had prepared her, somewhat roughly, for her upward journey, and heaven was not a haven of peace at all. It was a roaring place, and she lay helplessly beneath it.

She lapsed into unconsciousness again.

WHEN SHE AWOKE, the clatter was almost as deafening, but the air was warm, instead of cold. *A helicopter,* she realized. *I'm in a helicopter. Why?*

But she didn't really want to know. Knowing took too much energy. Knowing hurt. She wanted to sink into the safe painless void again.

But hands, kind hands, this time, held hers, kept her from slipping away as she wanted.

"Laura," said a man's voice, taut with concern. "You're safe. Tim's safe. Everything's all right."

A warm mouth pressed her cheek. "Everything's all right. I'm here," he whispered, his breath soft against her skin.

Jarod, she thought. *Oh, Jay. You found us. You made it back.*

In a swift painful surge, the will to live came back to her. He kissed her again. The touch of his lips made her want to return to consciousness, no matter how much her body hurt.

She felt herself smiling slightly. His hand squeezed hers. "You're safe," he repeated. "Tim's safe. Everything's all right."

And it was all right, she thought. They'd survived, all of them. And Jarod had returned to them.

Her eyes fluttered open. She wanted to see him. If she could see him, everything would make sense again. The pain wouldn't matter.

But when she focused her gaze, she frowned in puzzlement. It was not Jarod's face above hers. The eyes that looked at her with such concern were not Jarod's clear gray ones. Instead, Gus Raphael's dark gaze met hers. Gus Raphael held her hands.

"Laura," he said, his gaunt face strained. "Are you all right? Can you understand me?"

She was so disappointed that she shut her eyes and turned her face away. "Where's Jarod?" she managed to say. The bandages around her chest were so tight that it was hard to breathe, hard to talk.

"Are you all right?"

"Where's Jarod?"

"On the ground. With the rescue party. We've radioed them that we've got you. They're turning back."

"On the . . . ground?"

"We were afraid the chopper couldn't take off. Jarod started after you on foot. Then, just before twilight, the fog cleared. We came for you by air."

"He's on the ground?"

"Yes."

She felt his face bending closer and turned hers farther from him. She wanted to shake his hands from hers, but felt too weak. What was Gus, unwanted Gus, doing here? And what had he said about her brother?

"Tim?" she asked, squeezing her eyes more tightly shut against the pain.

"Tim's fine," he insisted. "Maybe a touch of pneumonia. They've shot him full of antibiotics. To tell the truth, he's in better shape than you. What happened to you? How did you fall? Can you remember?"

She sighed tiredly. Now that she knew Tim was out of danger, all she wanted was Jarod. "A dog. A wild dog. It acted crazy. I chased it off. But fell."

"A wild dog?" Gus asked, appalled. "Did it bite you? Will you need rabies shots? I've heard that rabies shots are the very devil—"

"No," she said impatiently. "It didn't bite. I chased it off. How's Jarod? Did he make it back all right?"

"Jarod's Jarod," Gus said, impatience creeping into his own tone. "He looks like hell, but he's fine. He could live on an ice floe at the North Pole and eat nothing but penguin beaks, and he'd survive. Me? I've been worried sick."

"There are no penguins at the North Pole," she muttered. "Really, Gus."

"So who cares? He could live there and eat ice. *He* had it easy. *He* knew what was happening. Your sister and I . . ."

She turned back to him, opening her eyes and staring at him somewhat blearily. "My sister . . . How's my sister? How's Susannah?"

"Impossibly bright. Impossibly worried. I'd never imagined her getting emotional. About this, she got emotional."

"Does she know . . . ?"

"She knows you're safe, and Tim, too. We've radioed her. She'll be waiting for us."

Laura sighed and closed her eyes again. She tried to pull her hands away from Gus's grasp, but his hold was too stubborn. Why did he have to hover so closely, hang on to her in such a possessive way?

"Laura," he said, "What can I do for you? How can I help you? What do you want?"

"I want Jarod," she said.

She sensed his body stiffen. His hands tightened on hers almost spasmodically. *Oh, why should he care?* she thought tiredly. *And hadn't Jarod told him? He said he'd tell him.*

She didn't want to think about Gus. She didn't want to see him. She wanted to sink back into the oblivion of sleep until she could wake up to Jarod's touch and see his steady, dependable, beautiful gray eyes.

Gently Gus let go of her hands. She was grateful.

IT WAS THE NEXT AFTERNOON, and outside it was snowing again. The dim sunlight shone through the window of Laura's hospital room. Laura didn't want to look at the gray sky. She turned her face away.

"All right," Gus said, sitting on the edge of her bed. "Maybe I'm a glutton for punishment. Would it be too much to hope for a simple thank-you?"

Laura colored with shame. She'd been in the hospital overnight, she felt almost as good as new, but she hadn't given a thought to Gus's generosity. All she could think about was Tim and Jarod.

Tim, the doctors assured her, would be fine. She'd seen him herself, talked with him and was satisfied they were right.

Tim had told her in his halting way that maybe the whole misadventure had been for the best. He understood things he hadn't understood before. He was ready to face the long road to recovery.

Susannah was staying at Tim's bedside. She left it only to visit Laura. Gus, alas, seemed determined to hover over Laura. She had yet to see Jarod; she was edgy and unhappy, and she snapped at Gus. That was when he had made his remark about thanks.

His words had shamed her, and she had to admit she'd treated him poorly. "I'm sorry, Gus," she murmured, unable to meet his eyes. "I do thank you. I can never thank you enough. I'm sorry I was sharp. We owe...everything to you."

She wished, nevertheless, that he wouldn't sit on her bed. She'd mentally reserved that spot for Jarod.

"De nada," Gus said with shrug that seemed grudging. "It was nothing."

"It was everything. I didn't mean to seem ungrateful. If you hadn't brought Jarod, I don't know what would have happened."

At the mention of Jarod's name, Gus's face grew moody. He gave another expressive shrug, and they sat in silence for a long uncomfortable moment.

He was dressed immaculately as usual: a white button-down shirt, an olive-green wool blazer, a silk tie, tan trousers. He was a striking man in his way, and Laura had seen more than one nurse casting him looks of appreciative interest.

He had sent her two dozen red roses, which sat on her bedside table. He had brought her chocolates, expensive ones. They sat, unopened, beside the roses.

He had brought her a book to read, one of his favorites, he said. It was a novel of espionage. Spy novels bored her. She would read a few paragraphs, then her restless thoughts would drift to Jarod. She wanted to see him more with each passing empty hour.

"Jarod," she said carefully, not wanting to make Gus brood more than he was. "Is he sleeping?"

Gus's expression was partly resigned, partly bitter. "He came here to see you. The doctors wouldn't let him in. Visiting hours were over, and you were sedated. He went to your house and crashed. He hadn't slept for about forty hours—"

"And he'd been fighting the wilderness that whole time," Laura said worriedly. "Did a doctor look at him? Is he all right?"

"He's *fine*," Gus said, his upper lip curling in distaste. He touched his shirtfront. "I, on the other hand, have a broken heart. Is it true that out there with the bears and the moose you developed a thing for Jarod?"

Laura raked her hand through her curls. "Gus, there are no moose in Arkansas. Moose are farther north—"

"I don't give a damn where the moose are. I asked you a question. Do you imagine you feel something for this man?"

Laura sat up straighter. She raised her chin. "I don't imagine it. Yes, I feel something for him."

Gus rose, frowning, and threw out his hands in an exasperated gesture. He began to pace the room. "Laura, this is some...some aberration of your mind. You don't want Jarod. He's...undomesticated. The man could live on weeds and be happy. He's a loner. He's like somebody from... from another century. He'll head out into the woods and be gone for days. You wouldn't be happy with such a man."

She didn't want to hurt Gus, but she didn't want to mislead him, either. And she refused to be manipulated by his glibness. "I *would* be happy with such a man," she said with conviction. "He's an extraordinary man."

Gus stopped in the room's far corner. He turned and looked at her, his face sober. "He's a throwback. Excuse me for saying it, but the man has no social skills. He's Tarzan. I know you. You're not Jane. You're not meant to live in a tree with Boy and Cheetah."

"You don't know me," Laura said in despair. "You never knew me, and I never knew you."

"I *know* you," he argued. "For years now. A few days in the woods, and you think you know him? You don't. He's not ready for commitment. He's a maverick. He'll never be ready."

"Shouldn't he be the one telling me this?" Laura challenged.

"You'll see," he warned. "Out of the woods, the magic'll wear off fast. Actually living with a man like that? And him, living with a woman like you? It'd never work."

She stared at him unhappily. His conviction seemed so certain it shook her. He was almost, but not quite, making her doubt her own lofty conviction. She fought off the feeling.

"Gus," she said, shaking her head, "he and I are alike. We're both...moralists or idealists or something. Maybe too much so. We both wanted to see the world in terms of black and white, even when it's gray. I need him to help me see right, and he needs me. I...we learn from each other."

"Some moralist," said Gus. "He stole my girl."

She sighed in exasperation. "I'm not your girl. And I realize that in Hot Springs you did what you had to do. I was hard on you. Too hard. But the rest of this...I'm sorry, but it's between him and me. I don't want to talk to you about it. He and I will talk about it."

"Will you?" Gus said, adjusting his perfectly knotted tie. "Think so? Jarod might have developed the hots for you off in the forest primeval, but back in civilization, he's going to get cold feet. He'll be gone before you know it."

"You don't know that," she challenged, hurt by the charge.

"Don't I?" His expression was both defiant and troubled.

"I think you should leave," she said quietly. "I'm grateful to you, eternally grateful. But I can't listen to this kind of talk. I just can't."

A look of stubbornness hardened Gus's complex elegant face. "I'll leave," he said. "But I'll be back. I promise you. Even your sister's pulling for me. She thinks this thing with Jarod is too reckless, too sudden."

"Gus, *please*," she said.

"Anything," he said. "For you anything. Even leaving—for now. He may not be back. But I will."

His face was rigid with control. Yet he blew her a kiss, an oddly touching gesture. Then he turned and was gone, favoring his bad foot.

Jarod, come to me, she thought desperately. *Walk in, sneak in, but come. Climb in through the window if you have to. But come, please.*

Gus couldn't be right, Laura had thought in angry confusion. He was just the same slippery old Gus, playing his same old mind games. A man like him could never understand a man of integrity like Jarod. He was jealous, that was all. Jealous and wrong.

But it turned out he was not wrong.

She did not see Jarod again. By the evening, he was gone. All he'd left her was a note.

Susannah brought it to her that same evening. She stood by Laura's bed, her hands clasped nervously before her, as Laura, frowning in disbelief, unfolded the paper and read.

Laura—
Many things happened to us. We should take time to think them over. I have to go. It's an emergency. I'll be in touch. Until then—

Best wishes,
Jarod

"Best wishes?" Laura cried, aghast. "After all we've been through, he just walks away and sends *best wishes?"*

Susannah shifted uncomfortably. "Well, I wasn't there when the call came. Somebody in Texas wanted him—it really was some sort of emergency—an elderly person wandered off into some bayou or something. Down around Orange, Texas. Authorities found out he was here and called him."

Laura looked at her sister unhappily, tears glinting in her eyes. "He just left? He didn't even phone or stop to say goodbye? This is *all?"* She gave the note a disgusted shake.

Susannah shrugged unhappily. Her smooth hair was pulled back more severely than usual, and her face was pale. Behind her large glasses, her eyes looked sad and haunted. She took a deep breath.

"At least he wrote a note. Apparently, for him, that's something," Susannah said, twisting her fingers more tightly together.

"I'm supposed to be grateful for *this?*" Laura demanded. "I've written warmer notes than this to people I don't even know. Why didn't he call?"

Susannah tilted her head and sighed. "I don't know. Maybe he doesn't like phones or something. Some people don't."

Laura was devastated. Angrily she brushed a tear away. "But didn't he say when he'd be back? Didn't he say anything else?"

Susannah squeezed her shoulder. "I only saw him for a minute. He hadn't even had time to shave. He looked like some sort of mountain man. All he said was to tell you he'd get back when he could."

When he could, Laura thought in furious misery. Everything he'd done reeked of the classic brush-off. They must "think things over." He must leave—for an undetermined time—and he would be "in touch."

She crumpled the note and threw it across the room. Susannah shook her head and went to pick it up.

Laura scrubbed another tear away, then crossed her arms, willing the tears to stop. She bit her lower lip hard. Then she looked at Susannah, who had an odd, almost guilty expression. She held the crushed note in her hand.

"Throw it away," Laura said with a fierce nod at the note. "Throw it in the trash where it belongs."

Susannah hesitated, then dropped the paper into the wastebasket. She straightened her back, as if steeling herself.

"Laura," she said, "I want to say something. I suppose Jarod seemed very... heroic or something, and it was easy for you to feel, well, infatuated."

Laura could not speak for hurt, sorrow and humiliation. She crossed her arms more tightly, as if protecting her very heart.

"Now," Susannah said, her voice slightly shaky, "Jarod's *interesting* of course, but is his a life-style you'd really want? Living in the woods in a...a cabin, I guess. With Jarod running off into the wilds everytime there was somebody in trouble? He's not like other people, Laura. You can tell it just by looking at him."

He's not like anyone else in the world, Laura thought, *And I love him. But doesn't he love me or want me?*

She fought against surrendering to her tears. She refused to do so while Susannah was there. She clenched her jaw.

"You're probably more tired than you realize," Susannah said. "You're not yourself. Jarod can't mean that much to you. You only knew him a few days. He dropped into our lives, and now he's dropped out again. But Gus, well, Gus has always been there for you. Gus *really* loves you. And he's a good person, a wonderful person—he truly is. You're very lucky, actually."

"Oh, if you think Gus is so wonderful, take him for yourself!" Laura cried, her patience snapping. "And let me alone, please. You don't understand, Gus doesn't understand—I don't think I understand it myself."

Then, to her chagrin, she burst into tears. Susannah came to her side to comfort her, but Laura waved her away. Susannah's face once more seemed more than a little guilty. She pressed her lips tightly together and left.

Once Susannah was gone, Laura found she had surprisingly few tears. Perhaps this time her sorrow was too deep to be assuaged by mere crying.

She picked up the hawk feather Jarod had given her, looking at it and turning it gently between her fingers. She had clutched it, a doctor had told her, even in the emergency room.

Maybe Susannah and Gus were right. Jarod was like the hawk, a wild thing, and he had flown away, off to another wilderness. After all, she told herself, he never said he loved her. Not once. And he had made her no promises. Not really.

He had told her sweet things, perhaps only to buoy her, to keep her strong at a time when she needed strength. Perhaps he had even meant them—then. But Gus was probably right. What need did Jarod truly have for her in his life?

Two years ago, when she'd found out the truth about Gus, she'd felt fury and loss and humiliation. Her anger at him was what had given her the will to go on and survive. But Jarod's absence wounded her so deeply she seemed to experience some sort of terrible death of the heart.

She sank back against the pillows and wondered if it would have been better if she had died on the slope of the ravine. She held the feather, because that was all she had left of Jarod. That and memories. And a note telling her goodbye.

She lay on her back, clutching the feather to her heart and staring at the ceiling.

Half an hour later, a nurse came in. "Your gentleman is at the desk—Mr. Raphael," she said. "My, but he looks as neat as if he just stepped out of a bandbox—and so exotic. He could steal any girl's heart. He wants to see you, even though it's not visiting hours yet. All right?"

"No," Laura said, still staring at the ceiling and feeling nothing, just the strange deadness of spirit. She could not bear to see Gus. Gus was the one who had brought Jarod into her life. "No. I don't want to talk to him. Not now. Not ever."

TWO DAYS PASSED. Ironically the hospital released Tim, but not Laura. She'd developed a cough and a mysterious fever that could not be brought down. The doctors feared that she, too, was going to succumb to pneumonia. One, more astute than the others, said she acted as if she didn't want to get well.

Susannah came faithfully to visit. Gus did, too, and Laura finally consented to see him. But when they were alone, there was nothing left to say. He seemed as uncomfortable and dissatisfied as she.

Several of the nurses teased Laura about Gus. They admired his looks, his clothes, his "sexy" accent, his gallant manners. Laura didn't respond. She looked out the window and said nothing.

The second day had almost ended and visiting hours were over when a nurse came to Laura's room.

"There's a most...uncivilized-looking man here," she said, her eyes wide. "He came barging in here, with your sister and your gentleman friend in tow, and he banged on the desk like a savage, demanding to see you and—"

Jarod! Laura thought. That single word infused her with elation. She leapt from bed, pulling on her old blue robe, not bothering to fasten it. She did not put on her slippers. She tore out the door, past the nurse, who stood with her mouth open.

Laura wore no makeup, her hair was tumbled, but she didn't care, for she saw Jarod. He stood far down the hall by the desk, and his stance conveyed all the coiled energy of a panther about to charge from its cage. She did not even notice that Gus and Susannah were with him.

She forgot she was angry with him. She forgot he had betrayed her. Nothing mattered except that he was there.

He looked terrible. His jacket was ripped and muddy. He wore his fringed leather boots, and the broad-brimmed hat, stained with dirt, was pulled down over his eyes. He was unshaven, his long hair loose and tousled. Yet, paradoxically, he looked beautiful.

"Laura," he cried.

Tears sprang to her eyes when she saw the expression on his face, heard him say her name. He met her halfway down the hall.

His hat tumbled to the floor when he caught her and crushed her in his arms. When she had first seen him, his face had been weary, but now it radiated life. "Laura," he said again, as if her name were a magic charm.

She threw her arms around his neck. "Jarod, Jay, you're back. Oh, you're back!"

"Of course I'm back," he said and kissed her hungrily. She became lost in that kiss, completely and happily lost.

When he drew away far enough to look down at her, she stared back raptly, as if he were a mystical vision. She could barely speak. "I thought... Your note... You didn't call— you just left...."

His expression grew guilty, pained. "They told me what you thought, Gus and Susannah. Laura, I *told* you I'd be back. Wasn't that good enough?"

"I couldn't believe it—you just left."

He held her more tightly, staring into her eyes. "I told you—it was an emergency. A seventy-nine-year-old man. Wandered away from his daughter's house and into the bayou. I had to go. I had to. It's my job."

"You found him?"

"I found him." He kissed her hair, then looked down at her again.

"You said we should think things over." Her voice was tremulous. "I thought you didn't want—"

"Oh, God," he said, pained, "I had to be sure you wanted me—with that business about Gus and everything."

"Wanted you?"

"Do you?" His clear eyes were so intent she wanted to die of bliss.

"Yes," she said. "Yes. And do you want me?"

He bent his head and captured her lips again, kissing her so deeply that her heart leapt, drumming a mad rhythm of happiness.

"Yes," he said against her lips. "Yes." He kissed her again. Then he drew back once more, taking her chin between his fingers. "Oh, Laura, I want you and need you. You make me feel connected to the world again. You do more than that. You make me feel whole. Will you come to Maine with me?"

"Yes," she said, locking her arms more firmly about his neck. "A camp should have a nurse. One who backpacks."

"It'll be a strange life. A crazy life. A little . . . wild."

"I don't care," she said with passion. "I love you."

His body went still with sudden tension. He looked at her as if she had spoken in a foreign language.

"I love you," she repeated. "Do you love me?"

The stern planes and angles of his face seemed to turn almost shy. "I . . . I never said that to anybody."

"But do you?" she asked. "Do you?"

He smiled, his smile crooked and a bit shaky. "Yes. I . . . love you." He lowered his lips to hers again. He whispered the words, as if savoring them, against her mouth. "I love you, Laura."

He kissed her until they both almost lost their balance. Jarod half-fell, half-leaned against a wall and laughed down at her in sheer delight. "Laura," he said. Then his face sobered. "Are you going to be well? Are you—"

"I am well—now that you're here. Oh, Jarod, why didn't you phone?"

He looked abashed. "I was afraid I couldn't leave if I heard your voice. Then I didn't know how to say what I had to say. I'd sent you the note. I thought it was enough."

"Your note was so curt, so short."

He shook his head and touched her face again. "It was the longest note I've ever written a woman. I thought I said all I needed to say. That you should think about if you really wanted me. I had to think of how to take care of you if you'd have me. I said I had to go—it was an emergency. I said I'd be back when I could. I meant it all, every word.''

"Oh, Jarod." She laughed ruefully, hugging him. "You may not say a lot, but you always mean what you say, don't you?"

"I try," he murmured. "But all this is new to me. Do I have to tell you things more than once?"

She shook her head and stared up at him, smiling fondly. "Yes, you have to tell me that you love me again and again and again. Every day of our lives."

He stared down at her, frowning slightly. "Can't I just show you? Like this?" Then his mouth was upon hers again, and the two of them were lost to ordinary reality.

"THAT'S DISGUSTING," muttered Gus, glaring balefully down the corridor at them. "Carrying on like that. This is a hospital, a public building. Carrying on like that. How can she forgive him—just like that? I begged two years for forgiveness. He didn't even have to *ask.*"

Susannah looked up at him warily through her big glasses. "I'm sorry, Gus. I guess they really do love each other."

He didn't glance at her. He kept staring at Jarod and Laura, and his face grew almost cold. He gave a nonchalant shrug. "Hey. It's the way the cards fall. But at least I finally did it."

Susannah crooked an eyebrow in concerned puzzlement. "You did what?"

He shrugged again and gave her an ironic smile. "I finally made her happy."

Susannah wanted to put her hand on the sleeve of his trench coat, but she did not. "Yes," she said, looking away from him. "You *have* made her happy, Gus. I'm sure she'll always remember that."

His expression grew more shuttered, more sardonic. "Come on. Let's wait in the car. I want to tell you something, *Miss* Finlay."

Her heart gave an inexplicable hop. "Yes?"

"I hope I've shown I'm a friend of this family."

"Certainly," she said. "We couldn't have asked for a better friend. We owe you everything."

"Right. You *owe* me. I put a lot of time and effort, to say nothing of my heart's blood, into this operation. And fair's fair. I don't intend to be noble about this—not altogether. It's not my style."

He took Susannah's arm. They started toward the elevator. She stole a glance at him. "We owe you?"

"Yes."

"Money? Laura said you were going to pay Jarod. You want money?"

"No." He said the word from between his teeth. "He won't take any money, the shmuck. Anyway it's not a question of money. It's a question of honor. I did you a favor. Someday I may ask one in return. And when I ask, you'd better say yes. Remember that."

Susannah nodded, feeling uncomfortable. He didn't speak again until they left the hospital and headed toward the car.

The night hovered halfway between mist and rain, and the streetlights had halos. Gus pulled his fedora farther down over his eyes. He kept Susannah's arm tucked in his.

"Why does this remind me of the end of *Casablanca?*" he grumbled.

"What do you mean?" she asked.

"I've just given up the girl. I'm in my trench coat, and my hat brim's pulled down. We walk arm in arm into the fog. Why do I have the irresistible urge to shrug it all off and say, 'This may be the beginning of a beautiful friendship'?"

Susannah's breath caught in her throat. "I don't know. Why?"

"I don't know why, either," he said, and then, because he was Gus Raphael, he laughed. "Just remember, Suzie-Q—you owe me."

"I'll remember," Susannah said.

IN THE HOSPITAL CORRIDOR, Jarod kissed Laura and she kissed him back.

"Do you think you could like Maine?" he whispered against her lips.

"Anyplace you are will be heaven," she answered, her voice tremulous with joy.

"Then let's go to heaven," he said. His mouth lowered to hers. He kissed her until her mind spun with happiness and desire.

I've found you, she thought, hugging him more tightly. *I was afraid you didn't exist. But you're real and you're here. And you're more than I ever imagined, ever hoped.*

"Love," he said, against her lips.

And she lost herself in the wonder of it.

* * * * *

*Find out how Susannah will pay back Gus
next month in UNDERCURRENT, a Harlequin
Temptation #485.*

**Fifty red-blooded, white-hot, true-blue hunks
from every State in the Union!**

Look for MEN MADE IN AMERICA! Written by some
of our most poplar authors, these stories feature fifty of
the strongest, sexiest men, each from a different state in
the union!

Two titles available every other month at your favorite
retail outlet.

In March, look for:

TANGLED LIES by Anne Stuart (Hawaii)
ROGUE'S VALLEY by Kathleen Creighton (Idaho)

In May, look for:

LOVE BY PROXY by Diana Palmer (Illinois)
POSSIBLES by Lass Small (Indiana)

You won't be able to resist MEN MADE IN AMERICA!

HARLEQUIN ROMANCE®

<u>Question:</u> *What will excite & delight Debbie Macomber's fans?*
<u>Answer:</u> *A sequel to her popular 1993 novel,*
READY FOR ROMANCE!

Last year you met the two Dryden brothers, Damian and Evan, in
Debbie Macomber's READY FOR ROMANCE. You saw Damian fall in
love with Jessica Kellerman....

Next month watch what happens when Evan discovers that
Mary Jo Summerhill —the love of his life, the woman who'd
rejected him three years before—*isn't* married, after all!

Watch for READY FOR MARRIAGE: Harlequin Romance #3307
available in April wherever Harlequin books are sold

If you missed READY FOR ROMANCE, here's your chance to order:

#03288 READY FOR ROMANCE Debbie Macomber $2.99 ☐

(limited quantities available)

TOTAL AMOUNT	$
POSTAGE & HANDLING	$
($1.00 for one book, 50¢ for each additional)	
APPLICABLE TAXES*	$ _____
TOTAL PAYABLE	$ _____
(Send check or money order—please do not send cash)	

To order, complete this form and send it, along with a check or money order for the
total above, payable to Harlequin Books, to: **In the U.S.:** 3010 Walden Avenue,
P.O. Box 9047, Buffalo, NY 14269-9047; **In Canada:** P.O. Box 613, Fort Erie, Ontario,
L2A 5X3.

Name: _____
Address: _____ City: _____
State/Prov.: _____ Zip/Postal Code: _____

*New York residents remit applicable sales taxes.
 Canadian residents remit applicable GST and provincial taxes.

HRRFM

Harlequin proudly presents four stories about
convenient but not *conventional* reasons for marriage:

- ◆ To save your godchildren from a
  "wicked stepmother"

- ◆ To help out your eccentric aunt—and her sexy
  business partner

- ◆ To bring an old man happiness by making him
  a grandfather

- ◆ To escape from a ghostly existence and become a
  real woman

Marriage By Design—four brand-new stories by four
of Harlequin's most popular authors:

CATHY GILLEN THACKER
JASMINE CRESSWELL
GLENDA SANDERS
MARGARET CHITTENDEN

Don't miss this exciting collection of stories about
marriages of convenience. Available in April, wherever
Harlequin books are sold.

HARLEQUIN®

Don't miss these Harlequin favorites by some of our most distinguished authors!

And now, you can receive a discount by ordering two or more titles!

HT#25409	THE NIGHT IN SHINING ARMOR by JoAnn Ross	$2.99	☐
HT#25471	LOVESTORM by JoAnn Ross	$2.99	☐
HP#11463	THE WEDDING by Emma Darcy	$2.89	☐
HP#11592	THE LAST GRAND PASSION by Emma Darcy	$2.99	☐
HR#03188	DOUBLY DELICIOUS by Emma Goldrick	$2.89	☐
HR#03248	SAFE IN MY HEART by Leigh Michaels	$2.89	☐
HS#70464	CHILDREN OF THE HEART by Sally Garrett	$3.25	☐
HS#70524	STRING OF MIRACLES by Sally Garrett	$3.39	☐
HS#70500	THE SILENCE OF MIDNIGHT by Karen Young	$3.39	☐
HI#22178	SCHOOL FOR SPIES by Vickie York	$2.79	☐
HI#22212	DANGEROUS VINTAGE by Laura Pender	$2.89	☐
HI#22219	TORCH JOB by Patricia Rosemoor	$2.89	☐
HAR#16459	MACKENZIE'S BABY by Anne McAllister	$3.39	☐
HAR#16466	A COWBOY FOR CHRISTMAS by Anne McAllister	$3.39	☐
HAR#16462	THE PIRATE AND HIS LADY by Margaret St. George	$3.39	☐
HAR#16477	THE LAST REAL MAN by Rebecca Flanders	$3.39	☐
HH#28704	A CORNER OF HEAVEN by Theresa Michaels	$3.99	☐
HH#28707	LIGHT ON THE MOUNTAIN by Maura Seger	$3.99	☐

Harlequin Promotional Titles

#83247	YESTERDAY COMES TOMORROW by Rebecca Flanders	$4.99	☐
#83257	MY VALENTINE 1993	$4.99	☐
	(short-story collection featuring Anne Stuart, Judith Arnold, Anne McAllister, Linda Randall Wisdom)		

(limited quantities available on certain titles)

	AMOUNT	$
DEDUCT:	10% DISCOUNT FOR 2+ BOOKS	$
ADD:	POSTAGE & HANDLING	$
	($1.00 for one book, 50¢ for each additional)	
	APPLICABLE TAXES*	$ _____
	TOTAL PAYABLE	$ _____
	(check or money order—please do not send cash)	

To order, complete this form and send it, along with a check or money order for the total above, payable to Harlequin Books, to: **In the U.S.:** 3010 Walden Avenue, P.O. Box 9047, Buffalo, NY 14269-9047; **In Canada:** P.O. Box 613, Fort Erie, Ontario, L2A 5X3.

Name: _____

Address: _____ City: _____

State/Prov.: _____ Zip/Postal Code: _____

*New York residents remit applicable sales taxes.
 Canadian residents remit applicable GST and provincial taxes.

HBACK-JM